G R JORDAN

Where Justice Fails

A Highlands and Islands Detective Thriller

First published by Carpetless Publishing 2021

First edition

ISBN: 978-1-914073-69-4

This book was professionally typeset on Reedsy.
Find out more at reedsy.com

The criminal justice system, like any system designed by human beings, clearly has its flaws

Ben Wishaw

Contents

Foreword

This story is set in Inverness in the north of Scotland. Although incorporating known cities, towns and villages, note that all events, persons, vessels and specific places are fictional and not to be confused with actual buildings and structures which have been used as an inspirational canvas to tell a completely fictional story.

Acknowledgement

To Ken, Jessica, Jean and Rosemary for your work in bringing this novel to completion, your time and effort is deeply appreciated.

Novels by G R Jordan

The Highlands and Islands Detective series (Crime)

1. Water's Edge
2. The Bothy
3. The Horror Weekend
4. The Small Ferry
5. Dead at Third Man
6. The Pirate Club
7. A Personal Agenda
8. A Just Punishment
9. The Numerous Deaths of Santa Claus
10. Our Gated Community
11. The Satchel
12. Culhwch Alpha
13. Fair Market Value
14. The Coach Bomber
15. The Culling at Singing Sands
16. Where Justice Fails
17. The Cortado Club

Kirsten Stewart Thrillers (Thriller)

1. A Shot at Democracy

2. The Hunted Child
3. The Express Wishes of Mr MacIver
4. The Nationalist Express

The Contessa Munroe Mysteries (Cozy Mystery)

1. Corpse Reviver
2. Frostbite
3. Cobra's Fang

The Patrick Smythe Series (Crime)

1. The Disappearance of Russell Hadleigh
2. The Graves of Calgary Bay
3. The Fairy Pools Gathering

Austerley & Kirkgordon Series (Fantasy)

1. Crescendo!
2. The Darkness at Dillingham
3. Dagon's Revenge
4. Ship of Doom

Supernatural and Elder Threat Assessment Agency (SETAA) Series (Fantasy)

1. Scarlett O'Meara: Beastmaster

Island Adventures Series (Cosy Fantasy Adventure)

1. Surface Tensions

Dark Wen Series (Horror Fantasy)

1. The Blasphemous Welcome
2. The Demon's Chalice

Chapter 1

Seoras Macleod turned off the shower and stepped onto the bathroom floor, where he picked up a towel and began to rub himself down. His muscles felt sore, and he partly blamed Jane, his partner. When she'd said he should get more exercise, Macleod had something else in mind rather than joining a bowling club. At first, he'd almost balked at the idea, wondering how your fitness could be improved from simply walking up and down a patch of green fabric, chasing a small, somewhat heavy ball up and down. Yet, now into his third week, he was finding that his legs were tired when he came in.

Of course, Jane hadn't accompanied him, and he felt it was more her idea to kick him out one evening so she could watch those programmes he didn't like. She had a habit for gazing at what Macleod would've called trash; investigations gone wrong, accidents waiting to happen, and any of the other reality TV shows that Macleod simply despised. In truth, he watched very little television, happier to content himself with either a book or simply a walk. This made him wonder why Jane thought walking up and down after a small ball was better for him than simply just walking.

'Company, socialisation, getting out there amongst people. You need to find a cheerier place,' she had said.

'I work amongst decent people,' Macleod had retorted.

'Yes, decent people who're doing the same job as you. Morbid, down-and-dirty job. A job that's bound to leave you affected. You need to talk to people who do normal jobs.'

Macleod had believed his job was normal. In fact, it had been normal to him all his life. It was the only job he ever had, policing. But if it meant he had to go out once a week to satisfy the love of his life, Macleod was happy to bite the bullet. Jane was often correct when it came to his mood and he wondered why she understood him so well, for many didn't. Stepping out of the bathroom, Macleod made his way through to the bedroom to wrap himself up in his dressing gown before making his way downstairs.

It was now half past ten, and hopefully, Jane would be finished watching one of her programmes and they could retire to bed. Once downstairs, Macleod went to the kitchen. He made himself a cup of hot milk, throwing just a touch of cocoa powder in, another one of Jane's ideas to help him sleep. It was true that milk had something in it that helped you get to sleep, but Macleod had always managed to sleep in his previous years. It was more recently that he'd been struggling. He thought maybe he was just old, at a point where he didn't need to sleep as much.

Old. He pondered the word. Never had he thought himself to be old. Yes, he'd gone from a point when he was no longer young, but old always sounded as if it was the end of the journey. Some sort of terminal forecast. Maybe that's what Jane was doing getting him out bowling, getting him to see life around him. Someday he would retire; someday he would not be a policeman. Macleod looked at the cocoa spinning around in the cup, and that's how he saw his career. Never ending, constantly spinning off one job to the next. He had no idea what he would do if he retired. Still, it was a few years off yet and besides, Hope wasn't ready yet. Soon, she would be.

Macleod left the kitchen, carrying his cocoa through to the living room, where he sat down at the end of the sofa where Jane had her legs up off the floor. Macleod saw a man on the television blabbering about some case and telling everyone that the murderer was still at large. Macleod gave a little shake of his head.

'Don't you start,' said Jane. 'I'm not having you do that. Just sit there. Don't listen. I'll be ready to come to bed in about five minutes.'

'I'm saying nothing,' said Macleod and stared into his cocoa. The hard bit was ignoring the sound from the television. He didn't look at it, but when somebody started talking about a case or about a murder, Macleod's antenna went into overdrive. What struck him was the fact that this was a local area murder, albeit it seemed to be from a while ago. Certainly, none of the names that were being mentioned struck home, but he was trying not to listen.

The telephone rang, and Jane looked over at Macleod, giving him a nod, indicating it was his to answer. There was no way she'd leave the television screen currently.

As he left, Macleod turned to her. 'What is this nonsense, anyway?'

'*Where Justice Fails*. Now get out,' said Jane, throwing a cushion at him. It was a good job he wasn't carrying his cocoa, thought Macleod. He made his way out into the hall to pick up the phone.

'Macleod residence. Seoras speaking.'

'Seoras, it's Jona, I'm afraid I'm going to need your assistance.'

'What's the matter, Jona?' asked Macleod, always anxious when he was called unexpectedly by the station's leading forensic officer.

'I've got a body I want you to come and look at. We're down in Inverness Cemetery. There's a disturbed grave and I've got a body on top.'

'You need me?' He was a little bit surprised by this. Ross, his DC, or either of his sergeants, Clarissa Urquhart or Hope McGrath, could pick up this one. It didn't sound unusual. There were strange people who did like to dig up bodies. The fact they'd left the body lying there might help give a clue to who had done it, but the body was dead. It wasn't going to get any less alive.

'Yes, I need you,' said Jona, 'and I'm not able to say over the phone. Too many ears around here where I'm talking.'

'Okay. I'll be on my way. Give me about half an hour.'

'There's no rush,' said Jona, 'but you may want the rest of the team down once you find out what it's about.'

'I'll make that call when I get down,' said Macleod, although he suspected if Jona was asking, it might be a good idea. 'Have you got uniform with you, sealing the place off?'

'Yes, I have,' said Jona, 'and it's secure; there's no rush from that point of view. I just think this might be coming onto your desk.'

'Okay,' said Macleod. 'I'll be with you shortly,' and with that, he hung up. Macleod made his way back inside the living room, where the programme was just finishing, the end music blaring out from the television. Jane flicked her head round, took one look at Macleod's face and grimaced.

'You're off out then.'

'Yes,' said Macleod. 'Jona wants me.'

'Well, Jona can't have you. You're coming to bed with me.'

'No, it's for work,' said Macleod, and then stopped, watching Jane's cheeky face. She always did this. Every time Macleod was being serious, Jane could throw in some sort of innuendo suggesting that every other woman around wanted his body. In truth, he liked it. It was one of the main attractions about Jane, that she could stimulate him, make him feel alive still.

Jane came from the opposite end of the United Kingdom, Cornwall, about as far away from the Isle of Lewis as you could get and the way they'd been brought up was as far apart as well. Jane's mother had been quite hedonistic and there had been several fathers that Jane recalled, but with all that, her mother was a fiercely loyal woman.

Jane had been nothing but good for him. She'd also learned to handle being an inspector's wife. She'd even been the target for one murder and refused his apology, saying he never needed to apologise for what anybody else did to her. Macleod had seen that his work had brought her into danger, but Jane would have none of it, proud of her policeman.

'I'll not wait up for you. I bet you'll roll in at five in the morning, if you do roll in at all. Have you got a clean shirt with you, a change for the morning?'

'Took it in last week,' said Macleod, 'but thank you for it.'

'Well, you've got to look your best at all times, haven't you? You haven't got the looks like Hope who can rock a pair of jeans.'

Macleod raised his eyebrows. He wasn't sure he'd ever worn jeans in his entire life, but his partner was definitely right about Hope. Didn't matter what she turned up in, she always looked good.

'I'll see you later,' said Macleod, making his way upstairs, changing quickly and then heading for his car.

The drive to Inverness Cemetery was short but did involve crossing the Kessock Bridge with its expansive views out to the Moray Firth. In the dark, Macleod could see several ships with their cruising lights on and an aircraft taking off from Inverness Airport. There was something about here that was growing on him.

Inverness was now his home in a way Glasgow had never been. Having worked much of his life down in the second city of Scotland, Macleod had learned a lot, but he'd never settled. Maybe it was Jane's influence that was helping him settle here in Inverness, for he'd been alone in Glasgow, moving there after his wife had died. The pain of losing her, a suicide on the Isle of Lewis, meant that he struggled whenever he returned home, but Inverness had been a good start for him, a new one and one that had borne a lot of fruit.

Macleod parked his car in the cemetery car park and could see the forensic lights focused on a grave about halfway across the large plot of land. He walked along the paths, refusing to cross past graves, as much out of wanting to keep his shoes clean as from a matter of respect. Macleod wasn't disrespectful to the dead, but he saw a graveyard as just a collection of bones. For him, the essence of the person was gone, he believed, off to another life, so what remained really was ashes to ashes, dust to dust.

He saw a woman in a forensic outfit waving him over and making her way towards him. The hood came down and in the bright lights that were illuminating the local area, Macleod could see Jona Nakamura, a short, Asian woman who ran the forensic teams. Normally she was extremely jovial, but she had a serious face, so Macleod knew something was drastically wrong.

'Inspector,' said Jona. 'Thank you for coming out.' Jona was always formal to Macleod in front of other people, but the pair had shared some intimate moments. Jona had provided a sort of therapy for Macleod, and he for her. They would often meditate together and outside of Jane, Jona seemed to be the person he could confide in the most. She had a very calm demeanour—serious, but often happy.

'What have you got for me, Miss Nakamura?' asked Macleod, returning the official compliment.

'We got a call to here earlier tonight, investigated by one of my team, which led to a body that was sitting above an unearthed grave. The coffin's there, it's empty. They put the lid back on and they put the body on top.'

'How did they dig the grave out?'

'Quickly,' said Jona. 'It's been dug after dark. By the looks of it, someone's actually driven in with one of those small diggers, taking it off the back of a trailer, digging the grave out, doing what they needed to with the body and then driving off again.'

'Seriously?' asked Macleod. 'Somebody's brought a digger here? I mean, did nobody notice?'

'Apparently there was nobody on site, but you need to follow that one up. Interesting thing is we looked at the headstone and it's for a Gary Warren. Well, the person that came out from my team, to be honest, is a little bit excitable with these things, but in fairness to them they checked the records for a Gary Warren. We have him on file as he was convicted of murder some years ago, so we have an image of him which my friend cross-checked. Now, given it's a corpse and it's been under the ground for a while, as you can see, it's pretty cut up, so they wanted to check if it was indeed Mr. Warren. The body doesn't look like him from a first glance, but with the time that's passed that's not necessarily proof.'

'So, what did they do?' asked Macleod.

'They checked the hands, which you will see have started to degrade, but one of the fingers still seemed to have a good fingerprint on it. They took that and compared it that with fingerprints we'd taken. They didn't match.'

'So, who's that?' asked Macleod. 'Do you know?'

'No. I'm working on it but like I said, I think this may end up on your desk. I've looked around the rest of the cemetery; there's no other disturbed graves. And one other thing of note, Seoras. Come with me.' Jona took Macleod over to a forensics van and insisted he wear one of the white forensic suits before taking him towards the grave site. As he got close, he could see what looked like a sticker on the side of the coffin. There was a red circle with a red bar across it indicating a forbidden sign. But within that circle and sticking out of the top and bottom was the image of Lady Justice, the tall figure that stands above the high court in London. The woman was holding up the scales of justice and had a blindfold across her eyes.

'You're right, Jona,' said Macleod. 'This one's coming to my desk.'

Chapter 2

Macleod spent the next twenty minutes picking up the phone and calling his team before making his way back to the grave and studying it. He struggled to understand what was going on. Where was the body of Gary Warren? Jona announced that she intended to put a tent over the grave to protect evidence so they could work. Rain was forecast for later in the morning, and so Macleod stepped away and sat inside his own car. He got a hold of his phone and rang the station, where the duty sergeant put him through to the records department. There'd been nobody there, but the duty sergeant was wise enough to send a young PC running to assist the inspector.

'I want you to look into a case for me,' said Macleod.

'Yes, sir. In what way?'

'Just want you to pull the file and send me the basic summary. I'm looking for a Gary Warren, convicted of murder. Unsure yet what he did. That's the name, not sure how far back it is, but looking at the body I saw tonight it's got to be less than twenty years. In fact, probably less than ten, but it's before I arrived, so it's more than three.'

'Aye, sir, I shall go and do that for you.'

'And it's Seoras,' said Macleod. Ever since the force decided to drop the sirs and ma'ams and any titles, Macleod had struggled to get people to do this for him. His own team were getting there, but such was his reputation, all the young constables kept calling him sir.

'Seoras, sir. Yes, sir.'

Macleod shook his head, closed down the phone and sat awaiting the constable calling him back. There was a tap on his window. When he rolled it down, coffee in a paper cup appeared.

'Miss Nakamura said you'd be requiring this, sir.'

It was one of Jona's forensic officers. Macleod smiled, said thank you and decided not to chastise him for using the *sir* nomenclature. In truth Macleod liked being called sir and wondered why they ever got rid of it. As he sipped his coffee, the phone rang again. The young constable had pulled the record for Macleod.

'I've got it, sir, and I'm just sending through to your email at this time. It should give you a brief rundown. Do you want me to do anything else with it?'

'Not at the moment,' said Macleod. 'I'll get the team to investigate that. Many thanks for your help. What's your name?'

'McGovern. PC McGovern, sir.'

'What's your first name, McGovern?'

'James.'

'Okay, James, thank you very much, from Seoras.'

'Yes, sir. Not a problem.' And with that the phone was hung up.

Macleod looked at his phone and pressed the button for the emails. The signal wasn't that strong, but he waited until he saw a new entry in his email list, pressed on it and then punched the file. He was still amazed that the phone could do this, pick up a document and display it to you. He remembered when he started out having to go back to the record cards, and then the new computers had come in and changed everything. He wasn't a dinosaur when it came to technology, he just wasn't as comfortable with it as someone like Ross. Ross loved it, could work with it in a way even Hope couldn't manage. Macleod was thankful he now had Clarissa on the team as someone else who didn't work technology in such a smooth fashion.

Macleod read the case in front of him while he awaited the arrival of his officers. The tent had been erected over the top of the grave. When he saw a car arriving, he stepped out of his own and watched.

The car initially stopped in the car park, but then made its way closer, driving along the tarmac that led around the graves. Once it had got within fifty metres, he saw the car stop and Macleod made his way over. A red-haired woman stepped out with a leather jacket on and he noticed boots that stopped knee high. As he got closer, he watched her circle around the car where the driver's window began to roll down. She bent inside and the lights of the car showed her giving a kiss, which was long and deep, to the man inside. When they broke off and she gave a wave, Macleod smiled to himself. It was a long time since he'd seen Hope so happy. And even in his time working with her, he'd seen a few false starts with relationships she'd had, but this one seemed to be working. Car Hire Man was hitting the money.

'Well someone looks splendid.'

'Thanks, Seoras. Quite possibly one of the best nights out I was having. Sorry about the attire, but I came straight here.'

'Apologies,' said Macleod, 'but it looks like this is a goer.'

Hope McGrath walked over to her boss, and he could see her worried face. 'It's going to end up on our desks,' said Macleod. 'Jona was called today to a report of a body dug up. Uniform called her in just to routinely identify the body. One of her people managed to identify the body as not being the one from the grave it was dug up on. That body is missing, and we got a new one on top, as yet unidentified.'

'Who was the original body, then?' asked Hope.

'It was a Gary Warren. He was convicted for murder in the past. Jona's trying to find out who the new body is, but they managed to get a fingerprint off it, and it didn't match up to those taken for Gary Warren. The case happened when I was in Glasgow but I've just got the rundown of the summary here. They said they had some difficulty finding the killer. It's worth looking into in closer detail. I'll get Ross onto that when he arrives.'

'Do you think we could go and check the body?' asked Hope.

'We've already done it,' said Macleod. 'I went over with Jona. She's got the tent up as they're doing some forensic samples.'

'I really could do with going and looking at the body,' said Hope.

Macleod stared at her. 'Why? There's not a lot more to see. We got photographs. The only interesting thing is there's a sticker on the side with a forbidden sign with Lady Justice on it. There's some point trying to be made.'

'I could do with seeing that myself, Seoras,' said Hope.

'What's the matter?' asked Macleod.

'What the matter is, Seoras, is I'm bloody freezing. Look at me, I've got boots up to my knees. I've got bare thighs, a short skirt on, I've got a blouse under here that frankly wouldn't keep you warm in the Caribbean, and I've got my leather jacket. I want to get one of those forensic suits on.'

Macleod burst out laughing.

'What?' asked Hope. 'You pulled me away from dinner. He may have even been asking me something tonight.'

'Oh, asking you? You mean he's going to—'

'Yes, ask me to move in with him.'

Macleod's mind had automatically thought marriage, but these days things weren't done that way. He should know—he wasn't married himself. Jane had insisted on not being married and Macleod had given in.

'Well, good for you,' said Macleod. 'Glad to see it's working out.' Macleod looked at his partner and he thought she must be cold, but it was also unusual for her to get so dressed up. Hope was casual; She liked her jeans. She liked anything that was baggy or sloppy, but right now Macleod thought she looked the part. No wonder the man wanted her to move in with her. And then he chastised himself again. Over the few years he'd known Hope, he'd realised she was much more than just a good-looking woman. She was courageous, as the scar on the side of her face showed, one she'd got from saving Jane.

'You run along and get suited up. We'll make some excuse. I can see lights coming anyway.' Hope turned round and saw the lights of a taxi coming into the graveyard. It drove up close to Macleod and he saw Hope wait to see who would get out. The side doors opened revealing a fancily dressed woman with purple hair who dashed out of the taxi, followed by a man in a dinner jacket complete with cummerbund and bow tie.

'What's the deal, Seoras?' asked Clarissa Urquhart, marching over towards him. Unlike Hope, she seemed to be in enough layers that she could survive a Siberian winter, but saying that, she did look immaculate. Clarissa was a bit older than Hope and her days of wearing less rather than more were long gone, but she cut a heck of a figure, thought Macleod. Yes, she looked eccentric and over the top, but always with such style. Meanwhile, behind her, he saw Ross coming towards him, the man looking neat and crisp in this cummerbund and dinner jacket.

'Did you guys organise a night out without me?' asked Macleod. 'I was stood having cocoa when I got the call. Where have you guys been?'

'Well, if you're not keeping up with everyone else, it's not our fault,' said Clarissa. 'I've just been out with Als. Meeting his partner, lovely young man. Got a few drinks and that.'

'But he's got a cummerbund and that on,' said Macleod.

'Well, it was the wedding of a friend of mine. Well, Lou's friend,' said Clarissa. 'Als was just looking the part, and rather well, don't you think?'

'She insisted I wear this,' said Ross, 'and we'd had a couple of drinks, so we needed to get the taxi here.'

'Okay,' said Macleod. 'Okay. Hope, go and get your outfit on. I'll bring these two up to speed.' Macleod ran over the details of the case to Ross and Clarissa before they all made their way over to Jona Nakamura in the forensic van. Hope was now standing in a forensic outfit, but she didn't look any warmer for it, so much so, that Clarissa took off a large shawl she was wearing and wrapped it around the woman.

'You may not think you have the looks when you get older,' said Clarissa, 'but trust me, love, it's a lot warmer.' Macleod was happy with the banter the team seemed to be picking up. Clarissa had that effect. She was a lot more irreverent and had the measure of Macleod when it came to taking him on, whereas the others were very respectful in general—even Hope, who could throw in the odd barb when they were alone.

'Inspector,' said Jona, 'I think I might have something,' and she brought the four of them into the small forensic van. It was a tight squeeze, but Jona wanted the door closed behind her.

'I brought you inside because I don't want this going out on the wind,' she said. 'It looks like the body out there is a Kyle Forsythe. We've been able to identify him through the fingerprint. The thing is the fingerprint was picked up in the same case that Gary Warren was involved in.'

'Gary Warren was done for murder,' said Macleod, 'and not a pretty murder at that. Killed a child. You're saying that Kyle Forsythe was in there as well?'

Macleod saw Ross on his phone, spinning and reading.

'Yes, sir. Kyle Forsythe was one of the suspects. It seems he was ruled out for some reason. I'm going to have a look at that. Apparently from the small bit of the case we've got here, there was some difficulty in finding the killer. But I'll pull the file, get a proper look at it. I've got PC Nowak starting in the morning.'

'The Polish girl?' said Hope. 'She's quite young. If I didn't know you better, I'd say you were at it,' laughed Hope.

Macleod stared at Hope, hoping to get across the message that it was an inappropriate comment at this time. Ross's partner was a man and Ross had no interest in women in the physical sense. Macleod knew that Nowak would be there on merit.

'Any idea how Kyle died?' asked Macleod.

'Looks like he was suffocated,' said Jona. 'Held down

somewhere, mouth covered over. That's what I'm suspecting at this time. I'll need to get the body back to the morgue to get a full examination. Hopefully we'll be moving it soon.'

'Keep me informed,' said Macleod. 'Anything else we should know?'

'I'm going to get the sticker removed off the coffin. See if we can work out where it came from. I'll need to tie in with Ross.'

'Is it just a normal sticker?'

'Yes, Ross, it is,' said Jona, 'but probably done locally, I would suspect. We should see if we can trace the design. Most of these people, if it's done by electronic print, would still have the image somewhere.'

'Yes, I can chase up on that as well. I'll get Nowak onto it.'

'Sounds like she's going to have a busy first day,' said Clarissa.

Macleod took his team out in under the forensic tent. Once they were all suited up together the four of them stood around the grave, looking down.

'So, let me get this right,' said Hope. 'They've dug the grave up?'

'Yes,' said Macleod. 'So, we need to get on the CCTV, Clarissa. See if we can find a digger on the move. If there's a car or van attached to that, then we need to find the car.'

'Is there anything else that we're here for?' asked Hope.

'No,' said Macleod. 'I think that's it. Now we've all seen it.'

'Good,' said Hope. 'Because I'm freezing. You need to drive us all back as well.'

Macleod looked at Hope, pulled out his keys and threw them over to her. 'Go and get in the car, I'll be over in a minute.' Hope looked at him and then made her way, followed by Ross. Clarissa was on the far side of the grave to Macleod, but she watched him as Macleod stared at the side of the coffin, a forbidden sign with Lady Justice in the middle that kept staring back at him. He didn't notice Clarissa walk around, but he felt her hand on his shoulder.

'Not good, Seoras, is it?'

'The other two don't see it, do they?'

'No, they don't,' said Clarissa. 'That's a challenge. That's saying we did something wrong.'

'A digger, Clarissa. A digger and the sticker on the side, body moved away. The planning behind this is big, and yet—'

'You could manage this as one person,' said Clarissa, finishing his sentence. 'You could manage this as one person.'

'Yes, you could,' said Macleod. 'And one person is always harder to find.'

Chapter 3

Macleod stood up at the conference table, indicating it was time for the rest of the team to get about their business. After coming back from the graveside, they had gathered together to quickly run through what they were going to do. And now at one o'clock in the morning, they were making their way onto their respective jobs. Macleod looked out through his office window to the outer office where the rest of his team worked.

Hope was the only one absent, and she made an appearance some thirty seconds later, now wearing a pair of jeans and a black T-shirt, but still wearing the knee-high boots she'd been out earlier in. Macleod grinned to himself. It was funny how for such a good-looking woman, the last thing she wanted to do was to dress up in any classy sort of fashion . . . unlike Clarissa, who seemed to go over the top with whatever she wore.

Still, thought Macleod, they were his team, and they worked well. He thought he'd put a phone call in to the closest member of his team before he got down to work himself. Macleod picked up the phone and dialled his home number, where after three rings it was picked up.

'Seoras, so what's the deal then?'

'I won't be home tonight,' he said. 'I thought you'd still be up.'

'I was just about to call it a night. I know sometimes you don't get to the phone, but thanks for calling and letting me know. I'll just have to snuggle up to that large teddy.'

The fictional teddy that Jane joked about kept changing between a large stuffed bear and a rather attractive gentleman. On several occasions, she told Seoras exactly how Teddy had cuddled her in an attempt to wind him up, but Macleod was not for taking the bait tonight.

'Is this going to be one in the press?' asked Jane.

'I don't know. It's a bit of a weird one,' said Macleod. 'I can't really tell you much else about it.'

'It's not the one with a body that's been dug up from the grave?'

'How did you know that?' asked Macleod.

'It's been on the news. They're just starting to get some pictures through.'

'What do you mean, they're starting to get some pictures through?' said Macleod. 'What have they been saying?'

'Well, it's funny, Seoras, because earlier on tonight, I was watching that programme, the one you were hating, *Where Justice Fails.* They were dealing with the case of Gary Warren. They think he wasn't the killer. It was some other bloke they were talking about.'

'What other bloke?'

'Kyle somebody, I think it was. They were running through why it wasn't Gary Warren, but he was dead now. Got some illness or something, and died. So, this was all posthumous. They were trying to correct the case, but I found it quite interesting because it was all local. I think it was before you worked here, though.'

'Yes, it was,' said Macleod. 'You're telling me that we've actually got press down on scene there?'

'Yes,' said Jane. 'I'm watching the news at the moment. If you switch the TV on, you'll see it. It's a special report.'

Macleod wondered how they got the name of the grave, wondered how the news realised it was linked to the earlier programme. He rapped the glass window in front of him, and his whole team looked round. Macleod pointed the finger to Hope, waving at her, indicating she should come through.

'The news is just about ending, Seoras. It doesn't say much. It's just lots of pictures. There's the big tent. You can't see the grave or that. I mean, it's obviously Inverness Cemetery.'

'They don't have to say much. They just tied it to the programme. There'll be a repeat of that programme. Trust me.'

'It gets repeated anyway,' said Jane. 'Lots of these types of programmes I watch do. You know that. You're always complaining you've seen them before.'

But Macleod wasn't listening, his mind instead racing. 'Okay, love. Look, I'm going to have to go. This has changed things again. I'll try and call you tomorrow and let you know what's happening, but at the moment, I don't think I'll be getting to bed tonight.'

'Okay. Teddy will keep me company, don't worry.' Then Jane said in a much more serious tone, 'Don't fret on it, Seoras. Take it easy. You always get them in the end.'

'Bye, love,' he said and gently put the phone down.

'Was that Jane on the phone?' asked Hope. 'I mean, you haven't got any other woman you call love, have you?'

Macleod spun on his heel. 'No, I don't, and we have an issue. It appears the press have got wind of the grave, but more than that, they know who was meant to be in there and who is now there.'

'How the heck do they know that?' asked Hope.

'My thoughts exactly. But we need to be careful. Ross's new girl isn't here yet, is she?'

'No, she starts in the morning, but she'll be tight. You know Ross, he's careful. He wouldn't just employ anybody. And besides, you saw her record. Anytime you employ anybody you scour the detail. If there was the slightest thing, you'd have brought it up.'

'I do, but I miss things. But you're right, Ross doesn't. All the information that comes through here, we need to lock it down tight. Need to get a word to Jona as well. I don't like this, Hope. This quick, this early on. Jane was watching a programme tonight, *Where Justice Fails,* and it had the case on it. They were going through why Gary Warren was innocent.'

'Tonight? On the TV? Well, it's no wonder the press are jumping all over it. Bit of a coincidence though.'

'Too much of a coincidence,' said Macleod, thundering his fist on the desk. 'I'm not happy about this. Somebody leaked something through. Anyway, you and I need to make a move.'

'Down to the Forsythe household, I take it,' said Hope.

'Exactly. We want to arrive before the vultures get there. The poor woman will have a circus in front of her.'

'Do you think he was innocent though?' asked Hope. 'I mean, is it a possibility?'

'Well, Ross is looking into it to get more detail. From my initial scan, I mean, it's a possibility. It's definitely not a foregone conclusion.'

'Do you want me to tell the team then? Before we go?'

'Go in there now,' said Macleod. 'I don't think I'll do it myself. I'm a little bit angry now, and those guys don't deserve an angry face.'

'It never bothered you in the past,' said Hope. 'But okay, I'll do it. Need to get your game face on, Seoras. We'll get to the bottom of it. Don't worry.'

'I'm not worried. I'm just angry,' said Macleod.

He watched Hope disappear back into the other office and almost jovially tell the rest of his team about the information that may have been leaked. Once she'd done that, Hope picked up a phone, no doubt contacting Jona, telling her team to keep it locked tight as well. With that, Hope made her way over to the coat stand and threw on the same leather jacket she'd been wearing that night.

It wasn't fair, thought Macleod. There she was, out with her man, enjoying for once a good night out, finally getting things to work and then this job came in and took her away. He knew that feeling. Not that he and Jane had been up for some sort of hot night, but rather they would have just been in bed together, lying peacefully, backs up to each other.

Macleod grabbed his own coat, slipped it on, switched the light out in his office and grabbed Hope on the way out the door. He let his sergeant drive across Inverness until they got to the home of Kyle Forsythe. The house was easily identifiable due to the large number of media crews around it, including a van which had *Where Justice Fails* written on the side.

'Do you think you can get through there so we can park up inside that circus?'

'It's pretty thick with people,' said Hope. 'We might be better nipping in. I mean, how well known can you be?' smiled Hope.

'I think we're getting more noticeable after some of the cases we've done,' said Macleod, 'especially amongst the press.'

Hope parked up a short distance from the crowd and locked the car once they had got out. Macleod started strolling towards the house. As he reached the police line of a number of uniformed officers, he ducked his head, insisting that the press crew in front of him move aside.

'Oy,' said a voice. 'We were here first to film.'

'I've got business inside, son. Step aside, please.'

'I've got business here too. We're trying to film this. We haven't had a chance to catch the wife yet.'

Macleod stared up into the man's face. 'Catch the wife? What do you think this is? Her husband's just been murdered.'

'Easy, just doing my job.'

'And I'm trying to do mine.'

Someone beside the man Macleod was arguing with suddenly produced a microphone. 'Inspector, can you advise us how the case is going so far?'

Macleod looked at the microphone and said two words. 'No comment.' He pushed on through, but more microphones were thrust at him.

'I think we need a statement. People deserve an update on what's happening. The press has a right to know. You've got a missing body, haven't you? Inspector, a missing body. How does that happen? How did someone dig up a body and leave a new one there? When was Kyle Forsythe killed?'

Macleod turned on his heel and looked at them. 'No comment.' He turned back and walked away.

'Can we not get a word from your sergeant? She'd look better on camera than you would.' Macleod turned around on his heel again and stared at the man who had said it. It was true that Hope would look better on camera than Macleod, but he also knew what the man was saying behind it, as if Hope was some sort of dolly bird to be placed there making a statement. She was a darn fine officer.

Macleod walked up to the man, eyes staring straight at him. 'Detective Sergeant Hope McGrath will deliver a statement to you, in approximately three minutes' time. You will give her every bit of your concentration during that time. And after that, Sergeant,' said Macleod, turning to Hope, 'you will get these people beyond the end of the street. There will not be a camera able to focus in on this house. We will set a cordon on either end, and we will control who comes in.'

'You can't do that,' said a voice.

'I can and I will,' said Macleod.

'What for?' said another voice.

'The protection of the family. Too easy for someone to hide in a crowd like this. Sergeant, sort this out, please.' Macleod flashed a glance at Hope, who was grinning broadly. She followed him into the house, where a police constable let them in.

'I'm afraid Mrs. Forsythe is not in a good way. She's lying down on the couch. We've got a doctor with her at the moment. Not sure how much you'll be able to talk to her, Inspector,' said the constable.

'That's fine, I'll wait, Constable. Hope, if you don't mind, can you step outside and show those people what you're about?'

'Gladly,' said Hope. 'You can put me in front of the press anytime. I know how much you love it.' Macleod followed Hope out, as she stood in the middle of the lawn with all cameras now focused on her. The press were barely a couple of feet away, microphones at the ready, and Macleod stood behind Hope.

For the next two minutes Hope briefly outlined a short press statement of what had happened in the case so far but removed any of the names involved. She finished up with investigations were continuing. A reporter blurted out a question.

'Did the programme have it right? Was Gary Warren innocent?'

'Gary Warren was convicted of his crime in a court of law,' said Hope. 'I will not speculate on that verdict. What we're focusing on is who killed Kyle Forsythe.'

'The programme got it right, didn't it? It's a bit of a coincidence, isn't it? Them saying this.'

'We're not here to read into coincidences about what's happening. We're here to investigate,' said Hope, 'and that we will do. I'm not here to make random statements concerning the reliability or not of certain reports by a programme this evening. What we are here to do is to speak to a bereaved woman and I'll remind you to bear that in mind when you next put a camera or microphone in her face.'

'Just doing our job.'

'Indeed,' said Hope. 'Now the briefing is over, if you'd all kindly step back.'

'Nice boots, though, love,' said someone as the press pack was moved backwards.

Macleod saw Hope's face flinch slightly, but she kept her chin up as they disappeared.

'Bloody boots,' said Hope. 'I was on a night out, Seoras. I couldn't help it.'

'I didn't say you could. At least you didn't turn up in what you were wearing. At least you've changed.'

'Can you imagine that?' Macleod almost grinned. 'That's

them all back out of the way, Seoras. Should we go and see if we can speak to Mrs. Forsythe?'

'You did well, Hope, and yes, they will probably stick a picture of you in those boots, but what the hey. DCI will probably like it.' Hope punched him in the arm. Neither of them had a great view of the DCI, thinking him to be a little bit media-happy. Certainly, anytime he spoke to Hope, there was always a grin on his face. But Macleod stood and watched the press pack being pushed all the way back to the end of the street. Satisfied, he nodded to Hope to follow him inside the Forsythe household. After the preliminaries of sorting the press out, he was about to go to work to find out more about Kyle Forsythe and see if he had any enemies in this world.

Chapter 4

Macleod stepped through the living room door and saw a woman sitting on the sofa. In front of him was a man in the suit who announced himself as a doctor and advised Macleod that Susan Forsythe could be spoken to, but that Macleod would have to be gentle. The woman was suffering from anxiety of the press outside and the previous incident many years ago when her husband had been a suspect in a murder case, as well as his sudden death. Macleod nodded at the man and waited until he'd stepped outside of the door before closing it and turning back to Susan Forsythe. She was sitting in a dressing gown, pyjamas underneath, probably having been alerted to the fact her husband had died when she'd already gone to bed.

'My name's Detective Inspector Macleod. This is Detective Sergeant Hope McGrath, and we're here to investigate your husband's murder, ma'am. I take it you're aware he was suffocated at some point and left in a rather prominent position.

'He went out earlier on tonight,' said Susan Forsythe, 'because he didn't want to watch that programme that was coming on.'

'Did he say where he was going?'

'He just went out for a walk. Although a walk with Kyle could be an hour, it could be three hours. Sometimes he'd stop down by the pub. To be honest, it wouldn't have surprised me if he hadn't come back in until midnight.'

'Did he call you at all when he was out?'

'No. He doesn't even take his phone. Kyle doesn't like being disturbed if he's gone out for a pint.'

'Is there anyone else in the house? Someone who can be with you?' asked Macleod.

'My boy is upstairs. He was asleep before all this kicked off. He'll sleep through to the morning, cos he's like a log when he goes. I'll be here for him. My sister's down in Glasgow but she's on her way up.'

Macleod looked over at an officer sitting on the sofa. She had long brown hair, which was tied up behind in the ponytail. She looked quite young, and Macleod heard a whisper in his ear. 'That's PC Wallace, Seoras—she's family liaison.'

Macleod looked over at the woman, 'PC Wallace,' and he gave a nod to the officer. 'I take it she's been making herself useful?'

'Your officer's been fine, Inspector,' said Susan Forsythe.

'Forgive me for saying,' said Macleod, 'but you don't seem that cut up about your husband's death.'

'My boy will be, my boy is, or was, Kyle's pride and joy. He's my pride and joy too, Inspector. Kyle and I haven't really seen eye to eye for a long time. The murder case is what did it. There was a lot of talk about our relationship. People tried to put a lot of pressure on me to say that Kyle had done it.'

'Who put the pressure on?' asked Hope.

'The investigating officers at the time when they came. Maybe it's just their way of trying to see if I was telling the truth, but I was, you see, they couldn't trace Kyle, and they couldn't trace that Gary Warren either on the night when the murder happened. But my husband couldn't have killed a child.'

'As I understand it,' said Macleod. 'They found a knife by the child's body with the DNA of your husband and of Gary Warren. You said that your husband was with you that night. Is that correct?'

'I didn't just say it,' said Susan Forsythe, 'he was with me.'

'The knife was from your kitchen.'

'That's correct. Gary and Kyle were friends of a sort, at least good acquaintances. Gary had been around here, and he must have taken it. I never really liked Gary Warren. He was an odd guy, very strange. He'd been around that evening and then our knife was found at the child's body with both DNA on it. Gary Warren had no alibi. Nobody had seen him. Kyle had been with me. We'd been up in bed together. Was quite a shock when your officers appeared at the door, started asking questions; it's bringing it all back though, because the press in those days were like they are today, all over us. We didn't get a moment's peace. I don't want any of that. I don't want any of that for my son upstairs. He was too young then to really grasp what was going on. At sixteen, he isn't now.'

'He still would've been close to the top of primary school or leaving it, wouldn't he?' asked Hope. 'Surely he would've known.'

'Oh, he knew a bit,' said Susan, 'but now he'll know even more. He's a sensitive soul.'

Macleod's phone rang and he excused himself looking at who was ringing. Ross's face had appeared on the phone, so he decided to step outside into the hallway.

'It's Macleod.'

'Boss. I've been looking through the evidence in the Warren case. It's not as clear-cut as you think. I know it states that the DNA was on the knife, and it suggests that Susan Forsythe then gave an alibi to her husband but Gary Warren was only placed there by having the DNA on the knife. Susan Forsythe said she had cleaned that knife after. The thing was, there seems to be some confusion, about when that knife was there and when it wasn't. Initially, the knife had been washed having done the dishes, but then she retracted that, saying that she hadn't actually washed it and she must have been mistaken. That came after they'd found DNA on it. They reckon that Gary Warren had been putting a bit of pressure on her. In fact, the investigating officers weren't sure if Warren and she had anything between them. They certainly weren't able to prove anything but, in the court, the deciding factor was that she said that her husband was with her. It just seems a little bit dodgy to say the least. Kyle Forsythe was only eliminated on the alibi of his wife.'

Clarissa's voice chimed in. 'I do like these open calls, Seoras, don't you?' and she gave a little laugh. 'I contacted the investigating officers, had to get them up out of their beds, but hey, we're working. They said to us that they were convinced something was going on between Susan Forsythe and Gary Warren, but they weren't quite sure what.'

'Do you mean a physical relationship?' asked Macleod.

'They didn't know. They said she was very cold to him, almost too cold. Said she didn't like him. Almost had a hatred of him when she spoke. But when they spoke to Gary Warren about her, he had nothing but good things to say.'

'Okay,' said Macleod, 'we'll look at it, but I'll need to find out if he's got any other enemies in the meantime.'

Macleod closed down the call and made his way back inside. Susan Forsythe was on her feet and asked Macleod if he'd like a cup of tea.

'If you've got coffee, the inspector will take coffee,' said Hope. 'Should I or our liaison make it?'

'No,' said Susan Forsythe, 'I'll do it. Follow me, Inspector.' She walked towards the kitchen. Macleod was struck by how the woman strode and now she was upright, he saw long brunette hair falling down behind her shoulders and a wiggle that he could see could be quite enticing for a man. When he entered the kitchen with her, he found that Susan spoke directly to him and not to Hope.

'I guess you're going to have to go through all of that from before, Inspector. I wish you didn't, but probably better we do it now then before my son gets up.'

'What's his name?' asked Macleod.

'John or John-boy as his dad called him. Like I say, he's a sensitive sod.'

'Looking back on the case,' said Macleod. 'There were some rumours that you and Gary Warren had something between you.' Susan's eyes flashed up. 'I take it that wasn't the case?'

'I said it back then, there was nothing. Not that he didn't look when he came round. A couple of times he touched me, not in ridiculous ways. You know, the odd tap on the backside, stuff like that. I didn't let Kyle know. He could be quite jealous.'

'Was your husband a violent man?' asked Macleod.

'No,' said Susan, 'quite the opposite.'

'Did he ever lay a finger on you?'

'Where are you going with this, Inspector? There's really no need for it,' she said as the kettle boiled beside her. 'I'm afraid it's instant coffee. Are you okay with that?'

Macleod nodded and Hope jumped in. 'Was Gary Warren very physical?'

'He was a brute,' said Susan. 'You could tell that even after the case. It came out he had several girlfriends. Came out that he was rough with them, and that child, well, they never decided if he was a nonce or not, did they? He certainly was a killer though. Brutal the number of times he stabbed her.'

'Brutal indeed,' said Macleod. He watched as Susan's eyes stared straight at him. She had that thing about her, almost as if she was daring him to look at her, to admire her. It was the sort of thing some women did. Macleod realised that some liked to be looked at, some distinctly didn't like to be looked at, and a whole load in the middle didn't really think about it that much.

'How often was Gary Warren around here?'

'Mainly when my husband was here. The two of them would go and drink in the pub, sometimes together.'

'He was never here outside of that?' asked Hope.

'He was here a couple of times. My boy saw him.'

'What was he here for at those times?'

'Usually he would just drop by,' said Susan.

'Did he stay long?' asked Macleod.

'A couple of times I couldn't get rid of him but that's in the investigation. I told them that because my boy had seen him come in and my boy had seen him leave. Collaborated with what I said. Like I say, Gary Warren was a man who wanted something, but I didn't give him anything. I'm a married woman, Inspector. Well, I was then. You understand that, don't you?'

Macleod nodded and took the cup of coffee that Susan was

now handing him. She handed a cup of coffee over to Hope but never looked at her. Macleod sipped his slowly, the hot liquid nearly burning his lips.

'Shall we go back into the living room?' said Macleod. 'More comfortable.'

'Better here,' said Susan, 'we can get a proper look at each other.' Macleod wondered what the comment meant but he nodded and continued with a basic line of questioning about what Kyle Forsythe had done in recent years.

'A member of the rugby club,' Susan said, 'quite well-liked. Didn't really have any enemies. He worked as a bricklayer. Had no trouble from his bosses. Lived for his boy. His only wish was that his boy was going to take up rugby like him.'

'Where's the pub he went to normally for his drinks?' asked Macleod

'The Fallen Maiden—it's about half a mile from here.'

'Oh, I know it,' said Macleod. Although he had never been in it, it was a fairly reasonable bar. Little trouble had come from it in the past. After another five minutes of finding out that Kyle Forsythe did not have an enemy in the world, Macleod drank the rest of his coffee and indicated to Hope that they should step outside. Joining him on the lawn of the house, Hope watched Macleod stare at the far end of the street.

'I enjoyed that bit where we pushed them back,' said Macleod.

'Did you enjoy the bit with her?' asked Hope.

'What do you mean?' asked Macleod.

'Because she was flaunting in front of you, wasn't she? Very subtly but she kept turning to you, kept making sure you were viewing her. Didn't want to go inside to the living room. She's one of those women, Seoras.'

'I'm not allowed to say one of those women anymore,' said

Macleod. 'You need to be more specific.'

'She likes being looked at. She likes to be thought of as attractive.'

'How do you know that?' asked Macleod.

'Same way as you do, observation. Never once looked at me, always at you. Did you see the way she twisted at times? Making sure you got a good angle on her. Wouldn't want to go inside and sit down again. Couldn't have been much between her and her husband. He's barely in the grave and she's trying to pick you up.'

'Do you think there was anything between them back then?' asked Macleod.

'Puts a different spin on the conviction, doesn't it?'

'You might be getting a bit ahead of yourself there, Hope. They had DNA.'

'But he's only got an alibi from her, and that alibi changes. If she alibied Gary Warren, Kyle Forsythe is in for murder.'

'I wonder how she said it,' pondered Macleod aloud. 'I mean, if she'd turned around and told the courtroom that she really didn't like her husband, but she's still covering for him—she's still giving an alibi; it sounds even more genuine, doesn't it?'

'But if that's not true, and he's forcing her to, it could still come out looking like that.'

'We've done enough,' said Macleod, 'it's time we get on. Let's get back to the office and see if Ross has come up with anything yet, but I don't like it, Hope; in some ways, I feel like I'm being led down the garden path.'

'I know what you mean, Seoras; it's bothering me as well.'

'What's bothering me is the TV show,' said Macleod, 'because that seems to be leading the same way and I don't believe in coincidences.'

Chapter 5

Macleod pushed the last sausage around his plate, sending it through the yellow yolk and the tomato sauce that had located together in the far corner. With one fast swoop, he scooped up the last of it on the front end with the sausage before dispatching the entire collection down his throat with only a brief chew. He wasn't really keen on eating at this time in the morning; he would rather be in bed, but he knew after a whole night up, he'd need something to sustain him. Possibly he'd grab a kip later that afternoon, or even late morning, depending on how things were going. But right now, he thought about getting a shower before heading back to his office.

Hope had been sitting with him five minutes earlier, with her scrambled egg on toast. During that time, she seemed to drift off looking at the window, but in truth, Macleod wasn't much for conversation. When he'd asked her where she was, she'd simply smiled back at him and gave a little shake of the head. *Somewhere private then*, Macleod had thought, and he guessed who with.

It had been a shame to pull her away from what clearly was going to be a special night, but Hope wouldn't have had it any other way. She was always ready to step into a case and was determined not to let the team down. Macleod had been worried about her for quite a while, that she didn't have a rock behind her. He knew what it was like down in Glasgow when he was on his own, and the terse, morbid, and quite judgmental character he'd become. Now with Jane there, there was a reasonableness in Macleod, even if the tough exterior was taking a long time to polish off.

The canteen door opened and behind two night-shift police constables came Clarissa Urquhart, smart jacket on, a scarf around her neck as ever, and the currently purple hair seemed to be locked tight in position. Macleod wondered if women still used lacquer because if they did, he was sure Clarissa used it.

'Seoras, there's a call for you. I'm not sure if you want to take it, though.'

Macleod looked up with a curious face. 'Why ever not?' he asked.

'It's the producer of some TV show. I think he's trying to get a comment after finding the corpse at the cemetery.'

'You say it's the producer; it's not like a reporter or anything?'

'No, Seoras,' said Clarissa. 'He said he was the producer, a David Jones. Shall I tell him to go away?'

Macleod took a moment. It was strange that the producer was ringing. What was he looking for? The coincidence of the TV show having shown the exact case that was then presented to the team that evening was also bugging Macleod. If it was just a coincidence, fair enough, but the speed of the turnaround from the television programme—he doubted anyone could have watched the programme and then simply bumped off Kyle Forsythe. In fact, hadn't Jane been watching it with him?

Macleod struggled these days because programmes were on demand. You didn't watch TV when programmes were aired, you watched them when you wanted and Macleod no longer knew what was on and when it was on. It used to be very straightforward. *Dallas* was on every week. Everyone tuned in for *Dallas.* At least, that's what they'd said in the station. Macleod had never been one for the big shoulder pads that had been a staple of everyone's viewing. Nowadays, it seemed viewing figures were lower because everyone was watching exactly what they wanted or at least, what they felt they wanted. Maybe they were just watching all the time, fewer people doing anything useful. Macleod realised he was drifting back into that terse inspector he'd been down in Glasgow.

'I'll take the call, but he'll have to wait a couple of minutes,' said Macleod. 'If you could be so kind, Clarissa?'

Clarissa cocked her head to one side. 'Okay, Seoras. Personally, I'd tell him where to sling it.'

Macleod almost laughed when she turned her back. Whereas Macleod was constantly trying to rein in his temper, to try and be a dispassionate and reasonable officer, Clarissa was quite happy to throw her comments out here, there, and everywhere, but she was solid, and she understood people and was a great foil for Ross.

After completing his breakfast, Macleod pushed himself up from the table and made his way out of the canteen, up several flights of stairs, and into the team office before locking himself away inside his own personal space. There was a light flashing on his telephone pad and he pressed it before lifting the earpiece.

'This is Detective Inspector Seoras Macleod. To whom am I speaking?'

'Ah, this is David Jones. I'm the producer of the television show, *Where Justice Fails*. I was wondering Inspector, could I get an interview about what happened tonight? I'd be very interested in getting you onto the show.'

'On the show, sir? I don't think that will be possible. We're in the middle of a murder investigation. It would be highly inappropriate for me to be on the show as I don't comment on an ongoing investigation.'

'Well, indeed Inspector, but surely you could comment on the case before it, specifically the Gary Warren case. As you know, we were doing some investigative journalism and it seems to us there's a rather insecure conviction that was served on Gary Warren. We were wondering if you would be prepared to come on and comment about it. I take it you have read the case file by now yourself.'

'As I said, I'm not able to comment on the current case. The case you're stating is heavily involved in this investigation, in the fact that quite clearly, Mr. Warren is not where he was meant to be and Mr. Forsythe is now in his place. There may or may not be a possible tie between the two cases, but until I'm sure and I'm able to give an informed comment about that, I would say to you what I've said to most of the press so far, and that is, I have no comments to make. Thank you for your call though and . . .'

'Just hang on a minute. Maybe if I talked to your DCI, I think he'd be quite keen for you to come on. The public are quite annoyed about this one. Gary Warren killed a child, but it looks at the moment like Kyle Forsythe was the one who did it.'

'Why are you saying that? Have you got evidence that Kyle Forsythe did it? Have you got evidence beyond what the jury was considering?' asked Macleod.

'Well, it's very circumstantial what they saw, but I think it's an obvious point, Gary Warren was basically convicted on the word of Mrs. Forsythe. Pretty clear to everyone that she was covering for her husband.'

'Pretty clear to everyone except the jury,' said Macleod. 'You're speculating, sir. If you have new and fresh evidence, I suggest you don't put it on air, but you come here to Inverness Police Station and present it, where it will be assessed in the same fashion as every other piece of evidence to every other case is assessed.'

'Well, on that basis, sir, I'd be loath to come to you because it seems that the evidence brought last time convicted Gary Warren.'

Macleod realised he was going nowhere with this conversation. Maybe he'd been seduced by the fact that he was in his office and not standing at a crime scene, trying to push the press back.

'I would suggest, sir, that you stick to facts and if you have anything that relates to the case, that is new, and has not been heard before, that you bring it in to Inverness Police Station. Now as you can appreciate, I'm a very busy man at the moment.'

'As am I, inspector. We're trying to get another programme on air for the public.'

Macleod could see Hope waving at him through the glass that gave a view of the office of his team. She was indicating something about having to go. Macleod nodded before watching her run out the door.

'Mr. Jones, I would say to you that you really shouldn't put out any more speculative programmes around this case. It can be detrimental to the case when it comes to court. Jurors could struggle to be brought forward as the judge may think they had too much of an influence from you or rather your programme.'

'More like they'll be bloody well informed.'

'I'm afraid, sir, I'm going to have to go. It's been a pleasure speaking to you.'

'Did you catch the show, sir?'

'No, I did not. I'm afraid I was quite busy at that time.' With that Macleod wished him a good day and put the phone down. *Blimey,* he thought wiping the sweat from his brow. It wasn't often you got people that keen. The occasional press pundit would come through, ask this and that, but once they realised you were stalling, they'd go away.

He came out from behind his desk, walked through the door into the outer office, and shouted over at Clarissa sitting at her computer. 'Where's Hope gone?'

'Had a call through, suicide up at the Kessock Bridge. She's gone up just to give it the once over.'

'Anything untoward about it?' asked Macleod.

'Not so far, Seoras. She didn't want anybody else to go up. She said she's going through it quickly. Ross and I are pretty deep in on this, at the moment.'

'Have we gotten anywhere with these leaks?'

'No,' said Clarissa. 'I've just been down talking to some of the night shift. I went back up to the crime scene as well. I talked to everyone there. I'm going over to Jona's crew. I'm not becoming too popular at the moment.'

'I'm sure you've got the good looks and flair to overcome that,' said Macleod, raising his eyes.

'You're a charmer, Seoras, aren't you,' said Clarissa. 'I can see why you chose me for this job and not yourself. You might have the looks, but you're right, you don't have the flair.' She stood up, flung her scarf around your neck, and marched out of the room, smiling all the time at Macleod.

Macleod could hear a snigger and looked over to see Ross hiding behind his computer screen. 'That's enough of that, Detective Constable.'

'Sorry, sir. It's just one of those funny texts you get sent.' Macleod gave a huff and made his way back into his office.

* * *

The air was cold and looking up at the morning sky, Hope thought there could be snow in the clouds. She wasn't sure yet, as the day was only just beginning to come through, but she could feel the bitterness in the air and wished she had a larger coat and gloves on. As it was, she was in her jeans and leather jacket, and she zipped it up tight. This was a long way from the warm wrap of arms she'd felt the previous night.

In a lot of ways, she was ready to move in. She had known John, her Car Hire Man as the team insisted on calling him, for a couple of months now, and they got on like a house on fire. In truth, she had really been living with him. She'd been in her own house so little, one she shared with Jona, that part of her felt bad. Yet, Jona never complained and always seemed ready to push Hope off in the direction of John's flat. As Hope walked up towards the crime scene on the bridge, she felt the warmth inside of the image of John back at his flat. That was about the only thing that was warming her up at the moment.

'Detective Sergeant McGrath, you called it in?'

The uniformed sergeant on scene nodded. 'Come this way,' said the man. He was a good six feet tall like Hope and able to look Hope in the eye, which a number of the officers were never able to do.

'You really should have brought a big coat and gloves. We've been stood here all morning and I'm frozen.'

'What happened?' asked Hope.

'Well, we're trying to run through CCTV at the moment,' he said, 'but basically, she jumped. We've brought her up, but the body's still here on the bridge. Traffic as you can see is being diverted onto the other side of the bridge, but it's that time of the day, isn't it? Everybody's heading to work. Everyone can see.'

'Do we know who she is?'

'Yes, Samantha Taggart is her name. Schoolteacher, apparently. We've got someone over there at the moment doing interviews, but she lived alone. Unsure at the moment why she did this. Brought a rope, tied it to the bridge, put the rope around her neck, took a jump. The forensic officer said she probably broke her neck as soon as she got to the end of the rope.'

'Charming,' said Hope. 'As far as you can see, there's nothing untoward. Looks like a straightforward suicide.'

'Well, yes, but we're going to check the CCTV. In fact, we should have that soon.'

Hope's mobile rang and she took it out thinking about simply ignoring the call, but saw it was Ross on the other end of the line. Pressing the receive button, she put the phone to her ear and stepped away from the sergeant. 'Excuse me, I've got to take this.'

'Hope,' said Ross. 'I got something for you. I think you're going to need to see it.'

'What do you mean?' asked Hope.

'I just got a call from one of my friends. They've just been surfing on YouTube this morning and lo and behold, there's a video posted up on it. It's been taken down very quickly since, but it was up there for about half an hour and there's now copies of it circulating throughout the internet.'

'What's that got to do with me?'

'It's your jumper,' said Ross.

'She took a selfie? How did she post it? That doesn't make sense. Did she do it live or something?'

'No. I'll send it to you. You need to watch it, but I'm taking it in to the boss as well. I think it's connected with the Kyle Forsythe case, whoever she is.'

'She's Samantha Taggart. I'll get you an address off the sergeant and send it through.'

Hope closed down the call, returning back to the sergeant, where she took what details he had about Samantha Taggart. She sent them in an email through to Ross and then saw an email coming the opposite way, containing a video.

'Sergeant,' said Hope, 'You want to take a look at this.' Together they both knelt down on the bridge, while Hope pressed the play button on the video that appeared.

At night, the Kessock Bridge was well lit, but Hope saw that the stretch where the rope was currently attached to illuminated more fully by whoever was making the film. The device had been placed at the start of the film, indicated by several wobbles and a stray arm. Then a man stepped back away from the camera into the centre of the image.

Where his face should have been was a mask, a 3D image of Lady Justice. There was a faint red ring around the face and a red slash going across it, but Hope could see the eyes through the mask. The man, wearing a boiler suit, disappeared off screen before coming back with a woman over his shoulder. She was blonde-haired but didn't seem to be moving. Around her neck was a rope, the other end of which the man started to secure to the bridge.

Without ceremony, he turned and threw the woman over the bridge. The camera picked up the rope going taut and then suddenly pulling tight before moving back just that slight touch, indicating that someone had reached the end of the rope and then settled back into a balanced strain. The man in the mask glanced over before coming back to the camera and pulling open his boiler suit. The t-shirt he was wearing underneath had the symbol of a forbidden Lady Justice, the same one that had been on the side of the coffin in Inverness Cemetery.

'Bloody hell,' said the sergeant, 'that's murder.'

Hope's eyes were looking beyond the screen. Cars were passing on the other side of the road, most slowing down to see what was going on, but Hope ignored them. Inside she felt cold. One murder was always bad, one death, but when you saw someone with an agenda, it struck at your core. Hope had been there before and there'd be more on the way. As if on cue, she felt the cold breeze of air and the first snowflakes of the winter started to fall. Last night's dinner seemed very far away.

Chapter 6

The snow started soft and light, but after ten minutes it realised it wasn't doing its job properly. By the time Macleod arrived at the Kessock Bridge, it was tipping out of the sky. Macleod was wrapped up in his large coat with his Wellington boots on and was carrying a bag when Hope saw him approach.

'These are for you,' said Macleod. 'Get them on before you give me a briefing.'

Hope opened the bag and then smiled, as she took a large coat out from inside. Once she was inside of it, she pulled some gloves out from the pocket and smiled at Seoras.

'Jane has it too good, do you know that?'

'Something you might want to remind her of the next time you see her. I don't think she's feeling that way at the moment.'

Hope smiled, and it suddenly dawned on her that John might not be feeling that way as well.

'So, what have you done?' asked Macleod.

'Forensics on scene. We reckon that the video footage was shot from just over here,' said Hope, pointing. 'We're trying to get through the CCTV as well from the bridge, but it actually looks like the man parked off the bridge and made his way up with the body over his shoulder.'

'That's quite a display of strength,' said Macleod. 'Why would he do that?'

'Keep the car off the CCTV,' said Hope.

Macleod nodded. 'Still a heck of a risk. I mean, the bridge isn't busy in the middle of the night, but it's not exactly clear. I wonder, was he disguised or something? How did he do it?'

'Well at night, some of the other walkways are quite dark,' said Hope. 'I don't think he's walked up the pavement. I think he's gone out towards the access platforms. That's where he's thrown her from. If you wanted to, I guess you could move through the shadows away from the cars, especially when they're not that abundant.'

'Either way, he's done it,' said Macleod. 'I take it we have officers over at the house of Samantha Taggart?'

'Yes,' said Hope. 'Forensics are here. I saw Jona pitch up about ten minutes ago.'

'Well, let's go see her,' said Macleod, stepping forward, leaving footprints behind him in the snow. He had to hold his hand up to his face because the swirling snow was driving into his eyes, but he eventually made his way round to the forensic vehicle. Jona was at the rear of it.

'Ah, Inspector. Well, thank you. You've given me ten minutes.'

'I take it you haven't got anything further for us then at this time?'

'Only this. She was alive when she went over. She might have been knocked out; she might have been drugged but she was alive. I can tell by the damage done when the neck broke.'

'Brutal,' said Macleod. 'Why her? Who was Samantha Taggart?' As Macleod was talking to Jona, his eye caught something on the other side of the bridge. He saw several constables trying to move a vehicle on. A man was hanging at the back of it with a camera pointed towards Macleod.

'Don't look now,' he said to Hope, 'But we're being filmed. See if you can catch the side of the van—see if it says anything on it.' Hope turned away from Macleod and began to walk along the bridge, but then turned, walking across it. She motioned over to a constable, pretending to speak to him, while she took a quick look at the van. She made her way back to Macleod a minute later.

'It says *Where Justice Fails*,' said Hope.

'That's the TV company that phoned me this morning. That's the one that runs the show. What the heck are they doing here? Get them out of here.'

'Easy, Seoras,' said Hope. 'I'll go deal with it. You stay on this and I'll sort them out.'

Macleod nodded and let Hope march her way off towards the other side of the bridge.

On her arrival, Hope made her way up to where two police constables were remonstrating with the driver of the van from the TV show. A man in the seat beside the driver was sitting quietly until he saw Hope, at which point he opened the door and started to make his way around the vehicle towards her. One of the constables moved across asking the man to get back into the vehicle, but Hope advised that it was okay.

'Excuse me, sir. You're causing a blockage and you need to move this van. In case you hadn't noticed, half the bridge isn't working, and these good people here are trying to get to work. You are preventing that.'

'I was just wondering if you would have a comment. I spoke to your inspector this morning, but he was less than forward with his views. I just thought you might be more ready to speak to us. Clearly we have a line on this.'

'How do you mean you have a line on this? What do you know about this killing?'

'Same person, isn't it? We have the YouTube video like everyone else. It's quite clear what's going on.'

'Whether something is going on or not,' said Hope, realising she wasn't aware of any case details around this particular murder. 'I will not be making a comment. Kindly get off the bridge and let the good people of Inverness get about their work.'

'We're legitimately here. We need to be filming this. The public needs to know about it.'

'The public needs to get to work,' said Hope. 'If you don't move, I will arrest you.'

The man glared at Hope. She realised he was sizing her up and down several times. 'You didn't have that coat on earlier on.'

Hope's hairs on the back of the neck raised. 'How do you know that?' she asked.

'Your inspector brought the coat to you. Prior to that you were there in your jeans and your leather jacket. I thought that looks a bit cold, but fair play to you, you've got the figure for it. I mean, the coat's nice, but for the camera, I think the rest of it was really the look we wanted.'

'You're causing a blockage. Get off the bridge.'

'It's the thing about TV. Everybody wants their detectives to be sexy, but in real life, most aren't. Most are just ordinary people like me. That's why I'm behind the camera. That's why I make the programmes. But you, you could be out front. You've got that sexy look. From your track record, you know what you're about as well.'

Hope could feel the anger inside her, but she wasn't going to let the man win.

'This is it, the last warning. You don't get back inside that van and move in the next twenty seconds, you're under arrest, sir.'

'What? You're going to arrest us filming this so the public can't be informed?'

'Yes,' said Hope. 'I will arrest you. We will move this vehicle from the bridge to let the good people of Inverness get to work. Now move.

The man glowered at her. Like a lot of people, he wasn't quite Hope's height, and he had to stare up to her.

'Okay, you win, but trust me, we could deal with someone like you presenting. If this job doesn't pay enough, come with me. Maybe some nice black leather trousers, nice and tight, something grippy around the top.'

'Move,' said Hope. 'If you insult me once more, I'll put you in for longer on a sexual harassment charge.'

The man's face went sore. 'Okay, love. Okay. No need to get angry when somebody says you're good-looking.' The man disappeared back into his van. The cameraman climbed into the rear of the vehicle, and they started to move.

The PC who had been trying to move the vehicle on turned to Hope. 'Thank you. Personally, you should go after him. That was uncalled for. He was trying to date you.'

'Yes. Happens a lot but the last thing you do with the press is entertain them. Get this all on the move then. Let these good people get to work.'

As the van pulled away, a man in the car behind it, rolled down his window and shouted out to Hope. 'That's it, love.

You stick it to them. Well done.' Hope didn't look back, but merely made her way across the bridge until she re-joined Macleod

'Any trouble?' he asked.

'Man in the passenger seat, I'd be interested to know who he is' said Hope, pulling out her phone, starting to tap in the name of the programme into a search engine. When it came up with cast, she started going through the photos of the presenters, but she didn't recognise the man from it. She then went through the production staff and saw him. A producer, David Johns.

'David Johns, the producer, was out in the van,' said Hope to Macleod. 'Seems a bit strange.'

'He called me this morning. I'm not happy about this, Hope,' said Macleod. 'Something's wrong here. They're too close to this. Way too close.'

'You could get it blocked. See if we can pull the programme down.'

'It's not on the decent channels though, is it?' said Macleod. 'Jane watches it? It's on one of those stupid ones. I keep telling her don't watch police stuff. I can't sit and watch it with her and point out all the nonsense they talk.'

'He actually offered for me to present the show. Wanted me to be a host.'

'I can get that,' said Macleod.

Hope cast him a glance. 'What?'

'You're experienced. You know plenty about the job.'

'Thanks, Seoras. I thought for a minute, you were going to say something else.'

'Well, come on. Who will people want to look at on the screen, you or me?'

Hope nodded. Macleod was right.

Macleod finished up with Jona, before seeing Ross arrive at the scene. The man was wrapped up a coat but seemed to be moving with some urgency across the bridge towards Macleod.

'What's up, Ross? You could have phoned.'

'I was on my way out. Sometimes I just like to get a lay of the land and I was just going to tag base with Jona, see if there's anything on the body that might give me any more clues.'

'It seems pretty straightforward out here,' said Macleod. 'He brought her along, he dumped her off the edge, wearing his outfits. How are we getting along with that?'

'Well, my new Constable, Nowak, should be arriving in the next hour so I'm going to get back, get her onto it straight away. I'm afraid the nice tour of the place is going to have to wait.'

'Just right,' said Macleod. 'The man's wearing T-shirts now as well. He's got a mask. He's got a T-shirt. He's got stickers on the side of coffins. We've got to be able to find where this is coming from, Ross.'

'I'm on it, sir, but just be aware of something.'

'What?' asked Macleod.

'Well, if he's able to get this stuff, and if this starts going on the television, what's to stop other people ordering the same thing?'

'But you'll know it then, you'll know what shop has it.'

'No,' said Ross, 'it won't. All it needs is a digital scan. All they need, any of them, to print it out as a file. Once somebody copies it, that's it and I'm going to be tracing left, right and centre. I need to be looking for who has already done this.'

'Fair enough, Ross. You know your business with that. Is there anything else you wanted me for?'

'Yes, sir. Hope needs to hear this as well. What I need you to understand is, I've looked up Samantha Taggart, made some contacts around the address. Turns out she lived next door to a convicted murderer. Janice Daniels was convicted of killing her husband in the house next door to Samantha Taggart. Janice Daniels killed herself in prison.'

'Killed herself in prison?' asked Macleod. 'What way? What was the method of dispatch?'

'She hung herself,' said Ross.

'So, he's copying?' said Hope.

'Yes,' said Macleod. 'He's copying their method of leaving the world. He's re-enacting the justice. Those who were innocent who ended up dying in whatever way, he's making sure that happens to whoever he believes is the killer. What we need to know is why he thinks Samantha Taggart is a killer just because she lives next door. Is there anything in the case files?'

'I haven't got through them yet, sir. We only started this thing last night.'

'Okay. Ross, get back and get on it.'

'Do you want me to go over to the Taggart house?'

'No, go back, see your new PC, get working through the computer on that line.'

'I'll go over then,' said Hope.

'No,' said Macleod. 'We just had a TV crew out here. My face, your face, we're going to be on that damn programme, you wait and see. No, we'll send somebody under the radar. I'm sending Clarissa over.'

'How is Clarissa ever going to be under the radar?' asked Hope. Macleod thought of the purple hair, the rather eccentric dress style and part of him agreed with Hope.

'She's under the radar in the sense that they don't know who she is yet. May the Lord help them if they cross her.'

Hope burst out laughing. 'Sorry,' she said, 'that's pretty inappropriate, but you're right.'

Macleod picked up his phone. He dialled a number and waited, his lips becoming increasingly dry in the cold air.

'Seoras. It's Clarissa, what's up?'

'Sending you the address of Samantha Taggart. I need you to get in the car and get over to her house quickly. Get round the neighbours, find out who knew what. It seems that our killer thinks that she's involved in a previous case to do with Janice Daniels, who lived next door. Killed her husband apparently. I'll start to get Ross to dig out the case files and send them over to you, but get over and talk to the neighbours, find out if there's any suspicion that Janice Daniels didn't kill her husband. Find out if Samantha Taggart knew them and what she was doing with them, if she did. Move fast, Clarissa.'

'Of course, Seoras; are you okay?'

'No. That blasted TV show was here, getting my face on camera, Hope's face too. If they get in your way, shift them. You have my permission to do whatever, except punch them, of course.'

'You take away all the fun, Inspector,' said Clarissa, 'but I'll get you results, don't worry.'

'And, Clarissa,' said Macleod, looking up at Hope, 'if they offer you a job in front of the camera, don't take it.'

Chapter 7

Macleod had returned to Inverness police station, happy to be back in his office and out of the cold from which he had suffered out on the bridge. By that afternoon, the traffic was moving again, the crime scene tucked away to a small corner, and no one had seen the TV van that had earlier pulled up and begun filming the area. No doubt they would be back trying to catch images of the team again.

Ross appeared at the door of the office, tapping it gently with his elbow and Macleod opened it to find the man was carrying two cups of coffee. He placed one down on Macleod's desk, smiled at the inspector, and then exited, closing the door behind him. Even in times like this, Ross was prepared, handing out the coffee, making sure everyone was provided for. Macleod wondered, *Was he the wife he never had?* Jane certainly wouldn't be doing that for him and neither had his first wife.

Macleod stood for a moment. It'd been a while since he thought of her. A while since he recalled her to mind. Jane had seeped into a lot of spaces, spaces where during the day, he would simply drift off to. Part of him thought it was probably a betrayal, but another part told him it was healthy, just where he should be. Life moved on, and the first part of his life was what it was. He needed to keep going. Macleod heard his phone ring, made his way toward his desk, and picked it up.

'Seoras?'

'Hello, Jane,' said Macleod, recognising his partner's tone. 'What's the matter?'

'Have you got a TV? You need to get to a TV.'

Macleod switched on the TV on the wall, one he'd been cajoled into buying as a tool for work, as Hope had put it. He knew that some of the other departments would sometimes put the TVs on when there were big games, maybe when the Scotland football team was playing or the Olympics, but the TV had stayed off unless absolutely needed. Sometimes Ross threw things up on the screen during one of their meetings, but he was the only one who really knew how to work it.

'Just give me a minute; give me a minute,' said Macleod, slightly flustered, looking at the remote control in front of him. He pressed the red button. 'What channel?' he asked.

'Thirty-seven,' said Jane.

How did we get to thirty-seven channels, thought Macleod. *When I grew up, there was just a couple. Still remember the Who-ha at channel 4.* Macleod pressed the buttons on the keypad and channel 37 came up.

He was surprised to see his face, but he recognised the scene. He was talking to Hope and the snow was starting to fall.

'They took that of me this morning. What's going on here?' asked Macleod.

'They're doing a special, Seoras. He's coming on live to talk in a minute but this is a special.'

'Special about what?'

'It's Janice Daniels. Apparently, the woman on the bridge this morning lived next to Janice Daniels.'

'How on earth do they know that?' asked Macleod.

'Well, they said they got a bit of a tip. That's all it said on the TV, Seoras.'

Macleod's mind raced. He wondered where Clarissa was with following up where the information was coming from but then he remembered she was over at Samantha Taggart's house, trying to get information from there.

'How long's this been on for?' asked Macleod.

'Well, it's been going fifteen minutes. Your face has appeared several times. So has Hope's. I have to say, she looks good on it.'

'Well, she didn't ask to be on it either. Do you know their producer actually asked if Hope wanted to go on that programme and present it? Can you imagine?'

'She'd look great, Seoras. I mean, she's a lovely looking girl. I wouldn't mind seeing her on the programme. I'm sure many of the men folk at home would.'

'She's not some prim dolly to be brought out. She's a proper detective. One of the best,' said Macleod defensively, 'and one day she'll take over from me.'

'There's the father figure coming out,' teased Jane.

'Don't start on this one, Jane; just don't go there. These people have me rattled. I'm sick of this. I'm no pop star and I don't want to be appearing on the telly.'

'Just calm down, Seoras. They're just making waves, trying to boost their ratings so they can get another season. That's all they want. You came across very efficient today.'

'What do you mean efficient?'

'There was a shot earlier on,' said Jane. 'A view of you telling some people to move.'

'How did they get that?'

'Looked like it was from a camera phone. They were also doing some shots of that guy running around with the mask.'

Brilliant, thought Macleod. *This is all we need, somebody like this whipping them up.*

'Well, thanks, Jane, for telling me. I need to get back to work, love. I'll hopefully see you tonight.'

'Just go get it done as ever. I always tell you that I don't expect to see you until it's done.'

'Then I'll be as quick as I can,' he said.

'And that's the romance I look for,' said Jane, laughing before she put the phone down.

Macleod turned the volume up on the TV. The presenter was interviewing people from around the Inverness area, asking what they thought about the actions of the masked man. While some of them said they were quite shocked by what he had done, a number of people seemed to be saying that at least he was sorting out where the justice system had fallen down.

How on earth do they know that, Macleod thought to himself. *How can they stand there and say that? They weren't involved. They haven't gone to court. They haven't heard the evidence, just watched some TV programme and decided. Rank amateurs.* And then a thought crossed his mind. *But they are also the general public. Somebody's stoking this up,* he thought. *Someone is . . .*

Then Macleod's jaw dropped. He saw a shock of purple hair in the background, moving quickly through a police line. There was a scarf around the woman's neck, and she seemed to be moving quite forcefully through a police line. The camera was in close, not specifically on Clarissa but was in the general area, and Macleod could hear her voice.

'I need to get to see my mother. She's incontinent. I need to sort her out.' He watched as Clarissa shoved her way through and was then apprehended by a constable. She seemed to whisper something in his ear before making a show of thrusting him away and then marching off to the houses behind the police line. Macleod smiled. She'd get to the bottom of it, and at least she could still move about incognito.

* * *

Clarissa was not best pleased. She'd arrived at the flat late that morning but already there was a large crowd. The boss had told her about the TV crew that had accosted him on the bridge, and she could see them again. Slowly, she made her way up to the side of their van before crouching down beside one of the tires. Clarissa kept her head on the move, making sure no one was around and listened to the air escaping from the tire. Once she saw it was flat, she moved off with no one any wiser that she'd been there. She gave a chuckle. Sometimes she felt like a big kid.

Clarissa made her way through the police line, claiming her mother was inside one of the houses. She walked up to the second house in the small cul-de-sac and knocked on the door, holding her jacket open with her credentials just inside, making sure whoever opened the door could see them but no one else could. An elderly man opened the door, somewhere around eighty years of age, and Clarissa smiled broadly at him.

'Excuse me, sir. I'm Detective Sergeant Clarissa Urquhart. I'm here to ask some questions about Samantha Taggart who unfortunately passed away this morning. If I can step inside? I'm sure you're as sick as I am of this crowd outside.'

'Certainly,' said the man and Clarissa walked in, allowing the man to close the door behind her.

'I apologise for the manner of my entrance but I'm trying not to appear on any film. There's a TV camera out there and they seem to be picking up every action the police do.'

'You'd think they'd just let you get on with it, wouldn't you?' said the man.

'Absolutely,' said Clarissa. 'I take it this is your house, sir?'

'Yes. Well, I live in a little annex at the back. My son owns the house but he's not in. His wife, however, should be about. Janice?' he shouted loudly. 'Janice?' Clarissa watched a woman in her middle age suddenly appear, a crisp blue jumper on, and black jeans.

'What's the matter, Dad?' she asked.

'Police for you. I'm just going back to my cricket.'

'What cricket's on at the moment?' asked Clarissa.

'Caribbean,' said the man. 'Not the same, the cricket out there.'

He turned and looked at the window, and Clarissa matched his gaze to see the snow continuing to fall outside.

'You'll have to excuse my father-in-law,' said the woman. 'He's a little bit not with it. You know how they get.'

'He seems very with it to me,' said Clarissa. 'Invited me in quickly, and helped me keep a low profile.'

'Are you here about Samantha?'

'Yes, I am. I'd like to ask you a few questions about her.'

'I'll do what I can.'

'I hear she was a school teacher?' posed Clarissa.

'Yes, at the local primary, around the corner. They'll probably be able to tell you everything about her. If I'm honest, I'm not going to be able to tell you anything good.'

'Why is that?' asked Clarissa.

'Well, she's two doors along but she was . . . how do I put this politely?'

You don't have to put it politely at all,' said Clarissa. 'Just tell me.'

'She was a tart. A complete tart. One of those women that had everything hanging out, wanting all the men to look. Then when she got hold of them, she used them for all she was worth.'

'Okay,' said Clarissa. 'Can I ask, do you know that for a fact, that she had affairs?'

'I know for a fact she approached my husband. Ian's a good guy, but she didn't leave him alone for a good while. In the end I had to warn her off.'

'You actually went round and told her off, to keep her hands off your husband?'

'Yes,' said the woman. 'He told her as well. Told her he wasn't interested, but she'd come round here and the stuff she used to wear. It was ridiculous. Summer was the worst. You can see at the back here. You can see all the gardens right along if you're up in the top room. Same with all the houses—everyone can see in. It's not great but when you looked into hers, well, she was there in frankly, not a lot on. In fact, I would say next to nothing.'

'So, she sunbathed out the back?' said Clarissa. 'Nothing wrong with that.'

'She was starkers,' said the woman loudly. 'Waiting for all the men to have a good look. That's what she was doing. Several people spoke to her about that.'

'Do you know of any husbands or men who she seduced here?'

'You could try three along,' she said. 'He's a single man. He would know.'

'Thank you,' said Clarissa. 'I'll get down to the school as well. Much appreciated.'

Clarissa made her way down three doors and found the door being opened by a man in a wheelchair.

'Sorry to bother you. I'm Detective Sergeant Clarissa Urquhart. If you let me in, I'll show you my credentials. I'm trying not let anybody outside see just who I am.'

The man looked at Clarissa suspiciously but opened the door. As soon as he closed it, she presented her credentials to him.

'I'm here to talk about Samantha Taggart,' said Clarissa. 'One of your neighbours a couple of doors up said you might know quite a bit of information about her.'

'I knew Samantha. I saw that news as well. Doesn't surprise me.'

'How do you mean?' asked Clarissa.

'Must be a dozen wives after her. She was unreal, highly sexualized. She was looking noon, night, and day for that sort of thing.'

'I take it you didn't approve, then,' said Clarissa.

'No. You get me wrong. I was more than glad that she was. Look at me; I'm not much use to a lot of women. Things down below don't work that well. Takes a lot of effort and Samantha was someone prepared to put that effort in. We enjoyed a very physical relationship, but that was it. She wasn't worth talking to, wouldn't call her an intellectual. You wouldn't even call her a reasonable conversationalist. But I had needs, she clearly did too. We got on together as I have no one else,' said the man.

'Your name, sir?'

'Frank Jones. Used to be in the military. That's where this happened. As much as I didn't like her as a person, I was glad of her.'

'Do you know of anybody else that was seeing her, any other men with wives?'

'Try my next-door neighbour, though handle it sensitively. The wife went through the roof at Samantha but she didn't know a lot. I think he got in over his head, way too deep, but that's just an observation. I know Samantha used to be round there all the time when the wife was out. But like I say, keep it sensitive.'

'Do you know them well?' asked Clarissa.

'I do,' said the man. 'He is my friend.'

'Can you ring him so I can talk to him on the phone, so I don't have to go in to the wife?'

Clarissa thought this was wise on the basis that the man might speak more to her. Five minutes later, she had the phone to the ear, speaking to the gentleman next door. She asked if she could come in to see him or if he could pop next door, but the man insisted that they go somewhere else away from all the TV cameras. Football ground car park was what he said, and so Clarissa waited a few minutes before making her way out.

She was sitting in the football ground's car park underneath the Kessock Bridge looking at how much the snow was white, perfect, and not indented at all, until a car came sliding across it. Clarissa had parked around the corner and was standing on her own, starting to get cold. The car pulled up and the man inside opened the door, allowing Clarissa to get inside.

'Are you Alastair?' Clarissa asked.

'Yes, and you are?'

'Detective Sergeant Clarissa Urquhart as I said on the phone. Here's my credentials.'

'Well, first off, this is all on the quiet. You can check where I was last night because I was on shift in work, so it couldn't have been me that was dancing around on that bridge, but please check it in a quiet fashion.'

'That I will do,' said Clarissa. 'I just want to know about Samantha.'

'That bitch, she nearly ruined my marriage,' he said.

'I heard she was quite clingy?'

'Oh yes, wants every bit of you. Things weren't going well with the wife, so yes, we started doing it. She'd come in the morning when the wife was out at work. I'd come in from night shift and we'd get it on. She was something else, she really was. But then I said I wanted it to finish as it started getting risky and riskier. One time the wife came back and Sam was in the bedroom with me. I had to pretend to be asleep. The wife came in and nearly opened the wardrobe with Sam in it. As soon as she was out the door, Sam's jumping back into the bed wanting to get at it when the missus is downstairs. All got too risky, too crazy, so I said no, I wanted it to end.'

'And how'd she take that?' asked Clarissa.

'She's been blackmailing me to this day. Like I said, I was in work this morning when she was being thrown over. It wasn't me, but the Lord above knows I wouldn't have minded doing it.'

'Were you the only one she was blackmailing?'

'As far as I know, but it wouldn't surprise me if she had others. The thing is, when I said I didn't care about being blackmailed and I was just going to come clean anyway, she threatened to kill me.'

'Was it a serious threat?' asked Clarissa.

'If you saw the rage in her eyes,' said the man, and his hands started to tremble, 'you would begin to understand what you were dealing with. Oh, she could kill. I'm sure of it.'

'So, what did you do?' asked Clarissa.

'Did the only thing I could do. I kept paying her. The thing is,' said the man, 'when she said she'd kill me, I kind of half laughed, tried to joke it off, but she stopped me, pulled me up close to her, her hand on my throat. She said to me, "I've done it before, gotten away with it. Just make sure you understand that."'

Chapter 8

Macleod called a meeting for seven o'clock that night. He was ready to make his way back to the station, having nipped out briefly for a half-hour for something to eat. Jane had come down with a hot dish of stew and together they sat in her car, looking out at the Kessock Bridge from a small car park across the other side of the Moray Firth.

'That's not the first you've seen on that bridge is it?' asked Jane.

'No. The last one was Christmas time, but he chose to do it. This woman was murdered.'

'They're talking about more specials of that programme.'

'I'm not surprised,' said Macleod. He took a spoonful of his stew and chewed on it. 'This is good,' he said, 'really good.'

'It's funny how the snow covers everything up. Makes it look okay.'

'That's true, love,' said Macleod.

'Are you here with me?' asked Jane.

'You know what it's like. The mind's on the go. I'm worried about this one.'

'Why?'

'There's information coming out from the inside, but I'm not sure it's from anyone low down. It just doesn't feel right.'

'Do you know they had someone on the programme today?' said Jane. 'I take it you watched it the whole way through?'

'No, I didn't,' said Macleod. 'I watched the bit where Clarissa was shoving her way through a police cordon. That was funny,' he said dryly.

'If you had watched, you'd have seen some former Glasgow inspector throwing his two-pence in about each of the cases.'

'Who?'

'Inspector Gordon.'

'The man's an idiot,' said Macleod. 'He was run out.'

'They said he was retired on the programme.'

'Well, yes, he retired. He was basically told that he was taking retirement, or he was out the door. The man cocked up a dozen cases. They'll put anybody on that programme. I can't believe you watch it,' said Macleod.

'I'm glad I'm watching it now; you can't even keep up to date on all these things.'

'You do realise that this job I do, it's not glamorous. There's actual real trauma with it. You are aware of that, aren't you?'

'Do you think I'm simple or something?' asked Jane. 'I get to see the trauma, I get to see it in your eyes, and I get to see the way you are with some of these cases—of course, I do.'

Macleod slid his hand over, taking hers in his. 'Sorry,' he said, 'of course you do. It's just the case. You know what it's like when I'm working.'

'Too well. Here, give me the rest of that dish. You get yourself back.' Macleod nodded, reached over, kissed her, and then wrapped his arms around her, while she couldn't respond, holding the bowls on her lap. 'You're a good woman to me,' said Macleod. 'I'll try and make it home tonight.'

'Well, if you're after eleven, don't wake me,' she said. He nodded, opened the car door, and stepped through the driving snow into his own car. Twenty minutes later, Macleod was sitting in his office as his team marched through. He took up his seat at the little conference table he had, Ross nearest to the TV, Clarissa beside him, Hope beside Macleod, and Jona looking like a referee in between them all.

'Where are we at?' asked Macleod. 'Ross, Gary Warren case?'

'I've been reviewing it,' said Ross, 'and if I'm honest, there is a potential for a miscarriage of justice in there. It's going to be very hard to prove because of the role of Susan Forsythe. It all hinged on whether or not the jury really believed her and her side of events. If she was lying and protecting her husband, quite easily he could have done it. In fact, in some ways, he's probably a better fit for a killer, but it'll be a hard one to overturn.'

'It's not the only thing,' said Clarissa. 'If you look at the Janice Daniels case, I've got a similar cause for concern, but again, it's very hard to prove. Samantha Taggart was here, there, and everywhere with everyone. She was blackmailing one man, possibly more, threatened to kill, and also said she killed before. Could be possible that she was at it with Janice Daniels's husband, and then framed Janice for it. When he was found dead in the house, Janice claimed that she hadn't done it, had only found her husband that way. Yet they managed to find fingerprints on the knife that butchered him.

'There was also no trace of Samantha in the house. Janice Daniels said she woke up and she found a knife there on her hands, husband lying on the bed, blood everywhere. It was particularly gory. You could look at it and work out that there was a potential for Janice not being the main cause, especially with what I know now. Again, that's hard to prove in a court, because there's no way half of these men are ever going to come forward. Most of them still have wives at home.'

'Have we got anywhere with tracing down the masks, the T-shirts, or the stickers, Ross?'

'Nowak's been on it. She's making progress, phoning around everywhere, but, to be honest, I'm not sure it's going to be an online transaction. She's been busy, racing through data from people's sealed records all day, and she's not going home. We'll keep at it. It's definitely a line to go along.'

'Remind me to drop by and see her at some point. I haven't even said hello.'

'She's good with that. I told her you were busy. She knows we're in the middle of stuff.'

'The first murder,' said Jona, 'we all know was asphyxiation. Our victim died much in the way that Gary Warren would've felt like he was dying, with the fluid building up in his lungs. You couldn't really pump the lungs full of water or easily manage a similar death in that vein. The best thing to do would be to asphyxiate, and therefore, Kyle Forsythe would feel like he was running out of breath, in a similar fashion to the water filling up in your lungs.'

'Gary Warren died of influenza,' said Ross, clarifying what Jona was talking about. 'I spoke to Jona about this earlier on today; the lungs just filled up with fluid and he could no longer breathe. Kind of makes you think what these people are doing.'

Macleod stood up from the table, and walked over to the TV, switching it on, and asked Ross to fire up some videos he had.

'All take a look at this,' said Macleod, and he showed them twenty minutes of *When Justice Fails* programme they'd been on that afternoon. 'You'll notice that myself and Hope are getting a starring role. I want everyone else to keep a low profile. Clarissa got in and out without being noticed even though she appeared on the programme in the background, apparently looking for her poorly mother. There was also something else that floated across my desk.

'There was a complaint from the *When Justice Fails* team. One of their tyres was let down at the scene. For some reason, they're blaming it on the police—said a few of the PCs looked a bit suspicious.' Macleod turned and stared at Clarissa. 'Personally, I want to take a crowbar to the entire vehicle, torch it, and throw it down a cliff, but it's not helpful, Detective Sergeant.'

Clarissa's face had a deep look of innocence as if she was horrified that Macleod would even suggest she would do such a thing.

'Have you gotten any further finding out where the information is coming from? These guys are too quick, too on the ball.'

'Well, I spent most of the time out this afternoon tracing down your other leads and I haven't heard anything so far, as I told you earlier on in the day, but I will do. Not making a lot of friends though.'

'That's fine by me,' said Macleod. 'If I find out someone has been doing this, I'll hang them. I'll go for them.'

'Can I just say that we need to relax,' said Hope, and the team looked at her. 'We've got TV cameras around, picking us up, checking what we're doing. We need to relax. We know what we do.'

'In fairness, Hope, they are getting slightly on my nerves,' said Ross.

'And that's what they'll do,' said Hope. 'We need to ease down, trust in what we're doing. Personally, I think the Inspector is right, Clarissa. There's no need for that. They're out there doing a job, these guys, nothing more, nothing less. Might not be a job we like, but they're doing a job. They're trying to entertain.'

'It's not entertainment,' fumed Macleod. 'It's rank dangerous supposition.'

'Yes, it is, Seoras, but again, ease down. There's no need for it. These people are nobody. They'll not help us get to the bottom of the case. We need to keep more focus on who's actually doing it and what do they gain by it,' said Hope. 'Have we got some sort of vigilante? Because they'd have to be a heck of a clever vigilante.'

'They would, wouldn't they?' said Macleod.

'Yes. What if someone isn't passing the information out? What if somebody's just using the information they've obtained?'

'What do you mean?' queried Clarissa. 'Somebody on the force is getting a hold of this stuff and deciding it hasn't been done right and then just sorting it out, making sure people pay properly for their crimes?'

'That's exactly what I'm suggesting,' said Hope. 'We're talking about looking for information being passed out amongst our own people. Maybe we should be looking for the killer amongst our own people as well.'

'Not convinced,' said Macleod. 'I don't think that the person that's doing this was a former officer. Most of us have got gripes about the force, about what we do, but very few us—I don't think any of us—would attack it in this way, especially when we're talking about justice.'

'Do you think this person could have suffered an injustice themselves?' asked Jona. 'Is that why they're out to save the world? Should we be checking through names of people who have recently complained to the station?'

'That's a point. Add that to your list, Ross,' said Macleod. 'Let's keep at it but step it up. It just feels at the moment like I'm waiting for the next body so I can get a little bit more evidence and wind it in.'

'Do you think this TV programme is involved?' asked Ross.

'I'm convinced of it,' said Macleod.

'I'm not so convinced,' said Hope. 'It's a bit far-fetched to say they're doing this.'

'I didn't say that they're doing it, but maybe they're in league with someone. Push up their ratings while their vigilante sorts people out and gets his reward.'

'Just be thankful none of the cases have come back against us,' said Ross.

'How do you mean?' asked Macleod.

'Well, you said, didn't you, that your face has been put on camera, as has Hope's. Is that for later on? Are they going to question one of your arrests? Say you've got the wrong person?'

'They can try,' said Macleod, 'but I think my convictions have been generally watertight.'

'Everyone thinks that,' said Clarissa, 'but in reality, most aren't. It's a balance. That's why you are judged. That's why you have a jury.'

Macleod nodded. The conversation wasn't going anywhere so he turned round and dismissed the team, advising to check back in at eleven o'clock that night. As everyone left, Hope remained. When the door closed, she spoke candidly to

Macleod.

'I think you're getting a little too riled up. They're in under your skin, Seoras.'

'It's not that, Hope. I'm convinced somebody in that TV crew is working with them, the murderer. How do they know all these stories? How are they tied in? You wait and see, there'll be another one and they'll be on it as well.'

'You think somebody's what, planning these? Actually, staging them? Make a programme and then killing off the free suspects?'

'No. No way,' said Macleod. 'Not like that, but maybe they're getting told about the cases from someone else and they're following it. A little bit of pre-knowledge, able to work up an angle, so that when it happens, they're straight on it.'

'So, you're saying, Seoras,' said Hope, 'that on one hand, we're passing out information. On the other hand, they're receiving it and then publishing it?'

'That's not far off it,' said Macleod.

'Well, if that's the case,' said Hope, 'we are in trouble.'

Chapter 9

Dennis parked the car and then clenched his fist open and shut, fighting through the pain that he felt. The longer he held the wheel, the stiffer the hand got, the harder it was to get it moving again. Beside him watched Sheila, her eyes full of concern, but he dismissed the way she was looking with a wave of his hand, announcing he was fine. It was time to get Alexis out, take her for a run.

Dennis liked the area just to the north of Aviemore on the A9, and the dog did too. Beside the road there were wide spaces, fields you could run through with no one around. There were no sheep in this locale, and if it started to rain, or even snow badly, they could always make their way into the wooded area about half a mile away. As Dennis opened the boot of the car, Alexis leapt up to lick him in the face. He saw Sheila put her hand down to her hip.

'Is it still biting at you, love?'

'It's never been right, has it? Need to have the op, get a new hip in,' she said. 'Eighty years of age and I'm reduced to this.'

'First it's the hands, and then that,' said Dennis. He drove because Sheila couldn't. When Sheila was forty, her hands started to seize and wouldn't let her flex them out properly.

She couldn't write anymore, tapping single letters out on a keyboard instead. But she hadn't let that stop her, and for that, Dennis loved her. She'd come out religiously every day, walking, trying to keep the rest of her body in shape. But the arthritis was spreading, and constantly some other bit started to feel more and more sore. Things just didn't work as well.

With Dennis, it was just his hands that couldn't form a proper shape to grab, but with some adjustments on the steering wheel of the car, he was still able to be mobile. He had driven them everywhere over the last ten years. That was the point of the dog as well. The black Labrador, faithful as anything, was a chance purchase but one that meant the pair of them had to get out walking. The dog didn't like to sit in, whatever the weather.

Today's weather was brisk, and there was certainly snow hanging in the clouds. For all that, there was a beauty here out in the mountains, south of Inverness. Dennis watched Alexis jump a fence and run with a blistering pace through the snow. It was untouched, deep, and he could see the dog fighting hard to lift her legs out of it and clamber through to the far end of the field. There was joy and exuberance, and Dennis smiled before looking back to Sheila who was now struggling along the road.

They would follow the road for at least a mile before cutting off onto a woodland path. By that point, Alexis would have run herself silly through the fields and come back to a more considerate trot beside her guardians. Dennis made his way to Sheila. Together they tried to clutch hands, but struggled, instead just accepting a loose hold, with a brief smile at the joy of companionship.

Dennis was watching carefully, for the road was mainly

white. No cars had driven over it, and it hadn't been cleared, being one of the lesser roads. They lived in Inverness, and having driven down along the A9, which had been cleared immaculately, snow resting at the sides, Dennis had been careful when he'd taken the turnoff and seen the white across the whole of the road. There'd been a minor slip by one of the corners, but nothing to get excited about. Still, it was worth it, and he breathed in deeply, taking in that fresh air.

In the distance he could hear a car, and the pair of them moved onto one side, keeping an eye on Alexis, who was still busy out in the field. A black Porsche drove past, and Dennis waved a hand up to the owner, for he had pulled wide, making sure he was well clear of them. They continued their walk, not hearing a car for the next ten minutes and began chuntering to each other about what they would have for dinner that night.

'You know I don't like ravioli,' said Dennis. 'You're always desperate to have ravioli. Why?'

'It's not the stuff that comes out of the tin, Dennis. It's nice. You know I like it. I find it hard to make though. I've not the hands for it these days.'

'Well, okay, I'll give you some help with it, see what I can do. Just as easy to buy the tinned stuff.'

'But where's the joy in that? It's tinned. I mean, that's the sort of thing you take out here, shove it in your pocket because it's easy to carry. You don't sit at home in a kitchen like ours and make tinned ravioli.'

Dennis laughed, and Sheila reached over, giving him a peck on the cheek. As she did so, her feet nearly went from under her, and Dennis grabbed her.

'It is slippery here; let's just be careful. Where's that dog got to anyway?' said Dennis, looking over at the field. The black

Labrador was now less black, and more a faint image moving amongst the snow. She had rolled herself in it, and the white had stuck to a large degree.

'Just let her be, she's having fun. Anyway, we can take it easy as there's something coming. Didn't you hear that?'

'That's a car,' said Dennis. He looked back down the road they'd walked along and could see a red car coming up. 'Easy, Sheila, into the side here. That looks like one . . . I saw that one earlier.'

'What do you mean you saw that one earlier? It's just a red car.'

'No, I saw that one. It was behind us coming out of Inverness. There's something on the bonnet. Hang on, why is he stopping?'

Sheila looked round and saw the car pulling over to one side. Behind the car they could see for nearly a quarter of a mile on what was a straight stretch of road. Ahead of them, it was the same. The car began to rev its engine.

'Don't know what he's at,' said Sheila. 'Call Alexis over. Don't want her running out anywhere near this person.'

The car engine continued to rev. Louder and louder it cut through the air like some sort of boy-racer at the starting line for a drag race.

'Where do they get these arseholes from?' said Dennis. 'I mean, seriously.'

'Just let him go past when he comes,' said Sheila. 'Don't wave your hand or do any of that nonsense you're prone to. Just let it be.'

'Let it be? Could do with booting him one right up the jacksie, showing off like that. Idiot.'

The car started to edge forward slowly. 'There's definitely

something on the front of the car, though,' said Sheila.

'I can't see from here without my glasses,' said Dennis. 'It's too far away. I mean, it's obviously the car that I saw before but the sticker's not that big, is it?'

'It's a quarter of the way across the bonnet. It's big enough,' said Sheila. 'Now behave. In tight. Looks like he's about to come up this way.'

The car was some three hundred metres behind them and slowly beginning to accelerate. 'Better stay in nice and tight, Dennis,' said Sheila, and the car picked up speed. Dennis was waiting for it to pull out, make a wide berth of them, but if anything, the car seemed to be hugging closer in to the side of the road.

'What's the idiot at? I'll get him to shift.'

'You do no such thing,' said Sheila. 'Don't antagonise him. Just let him go.'

'Can't let him go. Look, he's on a beeline for us.'

The car continued to increase in pace, and now only fifty metres away, Dennis realised that it wasn't going to avoid them. If it was, it would be at the last second. He turned and grabbed Sheila, trying to pull her off the road, and he flung her up onto the side.

The car continued apace, and Dennis turned around to see the car only a few metres from him. There was almost a difficulty in realising what was happening, as if this just wasn't right. Somebody, somewhere should be doing something about this, but Dennis struggled to do anything, and his hip was hit by the front of the car. He clattered up towards the windscreen, bounced off to the side and heard Sheila shrieking at him.

'Dear God, Dennis. Dennis, dear God, no.' She hobbled over

as best she could. As he lay at the side of the road, the car up ahead continued at pace, Sheila bent down to see blood across Dennis' face. He was barely moaning. One leg was at an angle that was not normal; the other leg was possibly broken as well.

'Dennis, what are we going to do with you? Dennis, where's your phone, we need the phone.' Sheila reached into Dennis's pocket where he kept his mobile phone. She was able to take it out, but her hands wouldn't work it, partly from the panic and partly from the arthritis that had crippled them. She began to cry, not tears of sadness, but tears of frustration and panic. She saw her dog leap over the fence and start running towards them. That was what caused her to lift her head and look up the road. It was then she saw the car had turned around. Once again, it was revving its engine. *No*, thought Sheila, *no!* The car started to increase in pace.

Alexis arrived, reached down and tried to lick Dennis in the face but Sheila shooed the dog. However, it would not run from its master, but instead as it heard the car coming towards him, stood in front barking loudly at it.

'Get out of the way, you daft dog, get out,' and Sheila realised she would have to run herself. She took three steps, leaving Dennis on the road. Shelia didn't look back, she had to keep going, just keep running. Her foot went from under her and Sheila landed hard, her chin splitting on the road but because of the ice and snow, she continued to slide into the middle of it.

Sheila used her elbows to roll over, and looking back, she saw that the car had just arrived at Dennis. Standing the other side of Dennis was the faithful Alexis. Sheila stared in horrified fascination as the car caught the dog full on in the face while the passenger side wheels ran over Dennis again. The car was jolted somewhat, especially from the impact of the dog, but it kept going, kept accelerating. Alexis was knocked to one side and Shelia heard her pet whimper, but she had no time to react as the car drove straight over her.

The wheels ran over over her legs, crushing them, and Sheila screamed out loud. She saw her dog whimpering, the head barely moving up from the rest of the body, which was failing to stand with its legs, two of them moving in a bizarre fashion. There was no sound from Dennis. When she looked along the road at him, all she could see was the blood seeping into the snow. Sheila could hear the roar of a car again, and it came up towards her. She tried to raise her arms up over her head to stop the impact, but as she did so, she heard brakes and the car screeched to a halt, stopping just a few metres from her. A door opened and someone came up close to her.

'Smile for the camera, love,' said a voice. Sheila looked up, her eyes blurred from her tears. There was someone there wearing a mask. It had that woman with the blindfold, the one you saw at the justice courts, but it had a red thing across her. Sheila's mind swam, unsure if she was hallucinating.

'Not dead yet. Well, there's always one more time.' The man in the mask turned and walked back to the car. It reversed. Then he turned it around and drove away from Sheila. She looked over and saw the mobile phone she'd had lying in the middle of the road. She wasn't sure if it still worked, but surely there must be some way to call someone. Sheila went to go for it, but her legs screamed at her, and she realised that she had nothing below her waist to move with. Her lower limbs were useless.

She drove her elbows into the snow on the road, but it was hard, having been driven over, and she struggled to pull herself along. The frictionless ice beneath her helped, but also meant that her elbows several times struggled and slipped, causing her to go flat onto her face again. Pain tore through her body, and she was still a long distance from the phone when she heard the car again. Sheila rolled over. In her ears were the whimper of a dog. *Why*, she thought, *why?* And the car got closer and closer. Before the car reached her, Sheila blacked out.

Chapter 10

It had been three days since Samantha Taggart had been thrown off the Kessock Bridge. Three days when that programme as Macleod was now prone to calling it, had appeared with numerous special editions. There was nothing new but a constant stream of justification for these murders. Barbaric as they were, the case was made that the people on the end of these punishments deserved no better. The papers had picked up the inflammatory statements being made, and the press was hounding Macleod's team like they were actual suspects.

The team was struggling for leads. Macleod had hoped that the digger used at the graveyard would have led them to someone. Ross had traced it through CCTV, but the car that had towed it had been found burnt out with nothing in it for forensics to find. The digger itself had been run over by forensics once they traced it lying at a roadside. It had been doused in petrol but had failed to ignite and Macleod reckoned that whoever was doing the destruction had been spotted, but no one came forward when the call was put out for a potential witness.

The small digger had been hired by a man in Muir of Ord

and it had been taken from the front of his house. Macleod had asked for the records of all those who were in the hire company and for those who had passed by. Had they seen anyone around? Every investigative effort had proved fruitless. Someone had stolen the digger and used it and then dumped the car and the digger. The car had been stolen from an estate on Inverness several days before.

The details surrounding Samantha Taggart were even less impressive. She had been in at home that evening but she'd gone out. Her car was found abandoned halfway to Aberdeen but from the moment she'd left the house, no one had seen her. One thing that was established was that she was a blackmailer and that she had several men who were happy that she was no longer around, although all seemed to have alibis. It was hard for them to go on the record for they wouldn't speak in front of their wives, but Clarissa, in her usual fashion, had dug deep and had managed to get the truth from most of them—private statements made that their wives would never see.

The trouble, Macleod had realised, was they had nothing while there was a growing clamour that seemed to see this killer as doing the public a favour. News programmes were debating the previous cases, generally without most of the evidence and Macleod was enraged. That was the trouble with social media these days, that none of the evidence was out there. Statements were being made by people that were just not factually accurate and Macleod was doing his best to ignore what was being said. He'd thrown it upstairs to the DCI and told him to sort that side, but all the while little titbits were being fed out to the press. That was what outraged Macleod the most. Clarissa was on it, and she was being thorough. Macleod reckoned she'd exhausted nearly everyone below her rank and indeed those at her rank. She was now going to have to look at those above.

It had been a gloriously sunny morning and Macleod had gone into work with a renewed optimism, but it was quashed when he'd heard about the killing. The first pictures he saw of it had been posted up on YouTube before the company had quickly taken them down. There was dashcam footage of a car driving at two older people and their dog, running them over before the camera was put in the face of the older woman. She had been taunted at, and then dispatched by being driven over again. The car had been carefully shot by the film-maker so that everyone could see the motif that was on it. Macleod was struggling to keep his cool as he watched it with Hope.

'How did they get that up there? How did they get that on?' asked Macleod.

'The company can't stop it, Seoras. It's the way of things. You know it, they're checking all these posts. That's not the only one. Then the trouble is, somebody sees it and they copy it across by the time they've taken it down. The company does what it can.'

'Well, it's not enough,' said Macleod. 'It really isn't. We can't have this. That's a snuff movie.'

'Okay, Seoras, okay. Look, I get it. It's been four days. I'm the same; I want to get this person now, but we haven't got anything.'

'No, and they seem to be getting everything.' Macleod grabbed his coat and headed for the car, Hope following in his wake. The drive down towards Aviemore had been completed in silence and when Macleod arrived, he found Ross was already on the scene. PC Nowak was with him but Macleod could see they had their hands full, for the press were there in abundance.

'Sir,' said Ross, waving over to Macleod. 'Let the inspector through,' Ross shouted, and Macleod nearly hung his head. He didn't want his arrival being broadcast and he could see several cameras being pointed towards him.

'Any comment, Inspector, about this latest tragedy? Who are these people, and why?'

'Investigations are continuing. Kindly step back,' said Macleod, keeping his head down and marching through.

'Sergeant McGrath, would you have any further comment?'

Macleod spun around and looked at a rather tubby man holding out a recording device. 'Sergeant McGrath has no comment either. Investigations are continuing. Did you get that?'

Macleod held his gaze at the man before turning away and marching off abruptly.

'Sir, this way,' said Ross, and he took the inspector some four hundred yards away before Macleod pulled him aside. He was careful to keep his back to the press and not look at Ross directly when he spoke.

'Don't announce me as the inspector. Don't announce my arrival, plus they've cameras everywhere.

'Yes, they had them on me when I arrived too,' said Ross, 'but I've driven them back quite far. I can't go any further, otherwise we'll start to block the road behind them.'

'You can go as far as you want, Constable, and I will back you to the hilt. Vultures.'

'Are you okay, sir?'

'No, Ross. I'm not,' said Macleod. 'I don't like this. I never liked the press, but this is beyond the press. Somebody else is pushing this, this agenda of the killer might be doing a favour to the general public theme. Every radio show you turn onto, every programme.'

'I didn't think you listened to many of those,' said Ross.

'I don't. I asked Jane and she told me.'

'Well, there's not a lot we can do about that now, sir, is there? So, let's just get on.'

'Yes, Ross. What were you going to tell me?'

'When I got here and I sorted the scene out and made sure we were secure, I spoke to one of the pressmen, a sort of friend I know from the past. He said they got a tip.'

'A what? A tip?'

'Yes. It said to be in the Aviemore area this morning.'

'When did he get this?'

'Oh, about maybe an hour before the incident happened.'

'Did he tell anybody?'

'Well, he phoned it into the desk sergeant but he didn't think much of it. I mean, it was a bit crazy. Nobody ever said who it was, it was just a random phone call. It's only when he got here with the rest of them, he realised that most of the rest of the press had got the same call.'

'The nerve,' said Macleod. 'Staging it, everything's staged. I really don't like this, Ross. There's something more. This is not just a simple vigilante; something's at work.'

'Well, we also dug into who these people are. They're the Gates. That's Dennis and Sheila. Got a dead dog as well—we believe it's theirs. The thing about them is that they were suspects in the case of a murdered dog-walker. It was a youth. According to the case notes, the elderly in his locale were having a bit of trouble with him. However, the boy was taken and he was raped and shot. Gun was never found, and Dennis and Sheila were taken in as potential suspects, interviewed, but released.

'Why were they released?'

'Well, the initial notes I've been reading through seems to release them because they couldn't actually place them there at the time. They had a loose alibi. However, if you go further into the notes which I've been able to do since PC Nowak had a look at them, she pointed out that Dennis and Sheila had arthritis to such a point they couldn't handle a gun. That's why they were ruled out.'

'Did someone get convicted?'

'Yes,' said Ross. 'A Martin Grass. Apparently, he was one of the elderly people who was having trouble. It seems he was a lot fitter than most of them, though.'

'But you said the boy was raped as well.'

'Yes. Martin was put away into a psychiatric hospital after he was convicted, and he also had a firearms licence for a gun. They were unable to trace the bullet that killed the boy to the gun because the bullet was never found but the wound size, everything, said it could have been fired from Martin's weapon. This seems rather strange because to me this conviction seems fairly secure,' said Ross.

'It does. The other two cases, there was at least some sort of justification for questioning them,' said Macleod.

Someone touched his shoulder. Turning, he saw Hope arrive. Macleod stepped back as he let Ross say again what he had found. Chewing over the thought, Macleod turned back to Ross. 'These comments about the hands, where did they come? You said it was hidden deeper in the case files.'

'Yes, it wasn't in the top summary. It wasn't even in the backup pages for that summary. It was quite deep, but it was certainly justified. There was no way they could have done this, what this vigilante seems to be accusing them of.'

'No doubt we can expect an entire precis about it in the programme later on today,' said Hope.

'We can,' said Macleod, 'and we'll make sure we see that we watch this, because I want to know if they get the story right. Because if they don't, it's saying something.'

'It's saying something?' said Hope. 'In what way? Do you think that the person who's giving them the detail doesn't really know it, they're not getting it directly, it's just snatched pages from somewhere?'

'No,' said Macleod. 'No, I don't. Who reads the summary?' asked Macleod. 'Who only skims the surface when they're looking into something?'

'What are you getting at, Seoras?' asked Hope. 'Ross, do you ever skim the surface on anything?'

'Not really. The devil's in the detail, isn't it? It's in the back of it,' said Ross.

'That it is. Do you ever skim the surface?' Macleod asked Hope.

'Only on those silly reports we get. You know, the housekeeping and stuff like that. Stuff that I don't need to know.'

'Exactly. You're in a management level. I skim certain things, not case files. Not about cases, but about other things. I don't think I've ever read fully the pool car documentation.'

'So, who would skim cases, then?' asked Ross.

'People high up in the force, people who don't need to know the detail. They just need to know this is what's happened, know there's going to be a public response, know when to have a few lines to say if this comes to press.'

'Seoras, you're not suggesting—'

'Clarissa is going to have to work harder on our leak,' said

Macleod. With that he walked off, making his way to where he suspected the bodies were still lying on the ground. Tents had been erected over them and he saw Jona at work with her team.

'Have you found anything?' Macleod asked.

'Give us a moment.'

'Sorry,' said Macleod. 'A little on edge, Jona. Just a little on edge. I want to get to the bottom of this. Did we find anything with the car?'

'Yes,' said Jona. 'Up the road, two miles, burnt out.'

'So, were there any tyre tracks around it? Any other cars?'

'No. It was taken off the road, set fire to.'

'So, the person who did this,' said Macleod, 'they would have had to walk away. Were there no footprints?'

'There were snowshoes,' said Jona. 'Prints of snowshoes beautifully disguising any tread.'

'But you can get a width, can't you, from it? From the impression of the snowshoe?'

'To a point, but you're going to be delighted to know that they're probably going to be average width and height if the snowshoe size is anything to go by. I can't be any clearer than that.'

'So, nothing?' said Macleod.

Jona shook her head. 'Sorry, Inspector. They're not daft, whoever they are.'

'But we've got somebody on the loose with a mask.'

'The mask was in there. It was burnt too,' said Jona. 'I'm trying to put back together what I can of it, see if we can work with Ross and find where it came from, but it's long work and it's not easy.'

'Okay,' said Macleod, 'again, we've got nothing,' and then he stopped, 'but thank you. You're doing your jobs and you're doing it well.' Macleod walked off.

'Is he okay?' asked Jona.

'No,' said Hope, 'He's not. Have you heard anything from the hospital?'

'They took Dennis in for surgery. It looks like they're probably going to save his life.'

'Is the Inspector aware?' Hope turned round and shouted. 'Inspector,' she said, aware that the press were not that far away and listening. Macleod walked back over. 'You do realise that Dennis is still alive.'

Macleod grinned. 'I thought he was a goner from the injury he sustained. They said it would be bad. Hope, I need you to get to Raigmore.'

'You've already got uniform up there,' said Jona.

'No, I want Hope there. I want Hope close by. It looks like we may have got lucky. He didn't finish the job properly this time. Maybe Dennis can tell us something.'

'It's hardly likely, sir, given the damage they did to him. I mean, the guy was wearing a mask in a car that he doesn't know.'

'That's right, Ross, but the trouble with something like this is they don't know what their victim knows so they'll make sure they can't talk. Get to Raigmore, Hope, and take care.'

Chapter 11

Hope sat in the coffee shop of Raigmore Hospital, a cold coffee in front of her as she bided her time waiting for Dennis Gates to come out of surgery. The man had significant injuries, and this was just the first exploratory operation, stabilising the man, who no doubt would have months of recovery and surgery ahead of him. Hope had seen many brutal killings in her time, but this attack seemed particularly vicious. To drive at someone and then repeatedly run over them again.

Sheila Gates hadn't stood a chance. According to Jona, the car had gone over her head during the second pass, crushing her skull. Her dog had to be put down due to the injuries it sustained. The sheer wanton brutality of the whole thing was getting Hope inside, but on another hand, she was feeling good about life.

John, her Car-Hire Man, had been a revelation for her. Finally, she felt she had someone who was supportive, not just simply after her to own her as some sort of possession. He was easy going, built her up, and so far, she was struggling to find a flaw in anything he did, except for his love of rugby. Hope wasn't particularly keen on the sport, but John was insisting that next time Scotland played at Murrayfield, Hope was coming with him. He'd even bought her a jersey, and she wondered, did she need a bobble hat and scarf to go with it? John said it might've been a bit more footballesque dressing like that. She had no idea what he was on about. As she was lost in these dreamy thoughts, from the corner of her eye, she saw her new partner walking into the coffee shop.

'John,' she said, waving her hand.

Her partner made his way over. 'Do you want another coffee?' he asked.

'No. This one's just sat here getting cold.'

'When you said you'd be here, I thought you'd be on duty around somebody's bed. Pretty nasty one from what I saw on the news.'

'Very nasty, but he's in surgery. I'm just waiting for the call and then I'll go back up. I'm afraid it's probably not a good idea if you come up once that happens.'

'All right,' said John, not used to this sort of thing. 'I just thought I'd pop round and see you. Make sure you're okay.'

'I'm fine,' said Hope, 'but that's a nice thought.'

'Like I say, it seemed quite a dark killing. I wasn't quite sure you'd be okay with it.'

Hope nearly laughed at the man. 'I've seen plenty and no, I'm not okay. At times, you'll get that from me in the quiet of a night or something. Trust me, John, I'll make great use of you when that happens, but day to day, I'm usually okay. If Seoras ever phones you, though, and says I'm not, you should get very worried.'

Hope wasn't sure if the man was grinning or a little offended, but she reached over, put her arms around him, gave him a large hug before kissing him fully on the lips. 'That's the extent you're going to get from me of that,' she said. 'I am on duty.'

'Yes, Sergeant,' he said. John had admitted to her the previous week the idea that she was a police sergeant was quite an exciting one for him. Although he'd stopped short of exactly how it excited him, Hope felt quite delighted about the fact. A lot of men felt quite powerless beside her with her height, her ability to take someone in hand, and also her determination, but John seemed quite happy to let her shine.

'Let's step outside,' said Hope. 'I think it's about time I got a breath of fresh air.'

There was a bench in front of Raigmore Hospital where Hope could see all the cars going in and out and look at the car park beyond. It wasn't the most romantic scenery, but as she sat on the bench with John's arm around her, she thought she'd rather be in no other place. Yet, something else was ticking away in the back of her mind—not about John, but something that Seoras had spoken about.

The TV, putting on a show. The TV would be there. It wouldn't leave her mind. She swore over the last six months she was starting to get more like Macleod, chewing on things. She often wondered if his mind was in any shape after the years of detective work he'd had, getting battered not just with the actuality of what happened, but with his own thoughts and guesswork.

John was muttering on about his day at the car-hire firm he worked at, and in truth, it was pretty dull. John realised that, and he spoke more about the characters that he worked with than about what had actually happened, but it was just a routine, humdrum day. As he waffled on, Hope took his hand, but her eyes were scanning the car park. A large van had just arrived and as she peered, she could make out the logo.

Where Justice Fails. She watched the van tootle along the car park, up and down, before finding a space. Thirty seconds later, a man she recognised as one of the presenters, as well as a cameraman, had stepped out and were making their way towards the hospital.

'Oh aye,' said Hope. 'You see them over there?' John stopped, looked over, and nodded. 'That's the TV company that is putting all this rubbish up. They keep trying to make out that we've cocked up in the past and that this guy's a vengeful killer, but he's doing the public a favour.'

'I did see it. I watched it because you'd talked about it,' said John. 'To be honest, I wasn't that interested, but I thought I would watch it because I knew you had a vested interest in it, just in case you talked about it.'

'What do you think of them?' said Hope, her eyes still on the camera crew.

'Well, it doesn't justify what he's doing, does it?' said John. 'I mean, how does it? I can't believe some of these people on the programme all standing there going on about how somebody did justice. I want to stand up and tell them, my Hope's in there. My Hope's going to sort it. Get out.'

Hope put her hand on his knee and squeezed it. 'I knew there was a reason I loved you,' she said. 'But come with me. I just want to keep eyes on these guys.'

John stood up and followed Hope, hand and hand, and together, they made their way in through the front door of the hospital, some ten metres behind the camera crew.

'They seem to be walking directly to wherever they are going,' said Hope. 'They haven't even asked where anyone is.'

'No,' said John. 'They're like men with purpose.'

'Well, I'd better see what their purpose is. Sorry, but I am on duty.'

She felt the squeeze of John's hand, and together they tailed the camera crew into the lift in the centre of the hospital. The camera crew slipped in first. Hope followed them with John, and she pulled him close, kissing him as the lift door closed. She didn't want the crew to see her face in case she put them off from what they were about to do. John reacted marvellously, pulling her in close, maintaining the kiss until the lift had stopped and the camera crew were on their way out.

'I do like this undercover work,' said John, and got a shush from Hope as they left. The camera crew were on the fifth level and Hope noticed they were making their way towards the operating theatre. They reached a door advising that they couldn't go any further because inside was where surgery took place and visitors were forbidden. The camera crew examined the door briefly before making their way to the other side of the corridor.

'Uh-oh,' said Hope, whispering in John's ear from a distance away. 'I don't like the look of this.' Hope stayed at the corner of the corridor, keeping herself and John out of sight. Every now and again, she would lean in to see what was happening. It was as she did this for the third time that she saw a man at the far end of the corridor wearing some sort of mask. He had his hands up in front of it, making it awkward to see, but Hope wasn't about to wait to find out if he was in trouble or not.

'Stay here,' said Hope, and took off, striding forward. As she got four steps around the corner, the doors of the surgery section opened, and a man was wheeled out on a bed trolley. At this point, the man with the mask dropped his hands and Hope could see the face of Lady Justice. She broke into a run.

A porter was pushing the bed along with a nurse beside him. The nurse screamed as the man in the mask yelled at her and held a knife above his head. Hope broke into a sprint. Seeing the man in the mask reach the bed and about to plunge a knife into the patient, she dived across the bed, catching him in the midriff and sending the man to the floor. The air was knocked out of her, however, because his hip had driven up into her stomach and Hope rolled away, gasping for breath.

'He deserves to die,' said the man in the mask as he got back up. Hope was behind him and wasn't going to have enough time to prevent him plunging a knife into the patient when she saw the orderly step round from behind the bed. The man caught the orderly with the back of his hand, then turned back to plunge the knife into Dennis.

And John was there, right in front of him. Hope saw him put his hand up, preventing the knife coming down, but the man in the mask then kneed him in the stomach before swinging the knife across, cutting John across the shoulder.

'No,' yelled Hope, now back on her feet and on the move. She snapped the attacker's wrist backwards and the knife fell from his hand, but she couldn't prevent him swinging his other arm and planting a fist straight into her face. She fell backwards but noticed that John, despite his wound, had reached for the knife and had wrapped himself around it. The man in the mask kicked him, but John didn't flinch, holding on tightly. Hope began to wobble back to her feet, but the man in the mask had taken off, running at full pelt.

Hope tore after him, yelling at somebody that there were casualties behind her. The punch he had delivered to her was a good one, and she staggered as she went along. She was still struggling from having had the wind knocked out of her and she sucked deeply every time she drew breath, desperate for more oxygen.

The man didn't head for the lifts, but instead went straight down the stairs. Hope followed him, every now and again shouting for security. An almighty ruckus was occurring, but it was behind her. Always behind her, not in front.

The man broke out of the ground floor emergency exit at pace, running over towards the car park. As he reached the road in front of the hospital, he scuttled across the bonnet of a car while Hope had to pull up short, negotiate her way past several cars and lost several yards in her pursuit. By now she was completely out of breath, running on empty, but she continued to run amidst all the cars in the car park to the fence at the far side.

She saw the man in the mask jump up, two hands on the fence and swinging his body sidewards, to get his feet up on top as well. Hope reached up and grabbed a foot, but she was prone for a counterattack and the man swung his other foot round, kicking her squarely in the face. Hope fell backwards and he disappeared.

She knew she was losing the battle, but regardless, Hope pulled herself to her feet, put her arms up on the fence and struggled to haul herself up and over. She flopped down on the other side, barely getting her feet down in time before falling onto her bottom. As she got up again, she looked along the wooded path and could see no one. Quickly, she ran towards the main road, but as she looked out, there was no one. Turning, she ran back down the path until it reached an estate, again with no one about.

She pulled her phone, dialled the police station, announcing that she needed cars straight away. She gave her location, gave how long the suspect had been running and demanded that the desk sergeant get things underway. It would be a long shot, but the man had to run somewhere. He had to ditch his stuff somewhere.

Realising now that she could no longer pursue, Hope suddenly thought of John. She saw the knife go across his body, saw him grip the knife when he went down to the floor and cuddle around it so that the man couldn't take it off him. In truth, John had probably saved the life of the patient, who was no doubt, Dennis Gates, but suddenly something inside her sank. Was John all right? How bad was the wound he received? Hope began to run back to the fence, hauling herself up and over. She raced back inside the building, and not waiting for the lift, she took each flight of stairs. Struggling, she got towards the fifth floor, hauling her legs which were betraying her, the lactic infiltrating them. When she got to the correct floor, she saw John sitting up against the wall, a myriad of bandages around him. An orderly was sitting with him, and a doctor was standing, looking down.

'How is he? How is he?' asked Hope, running in.

'And you are?'

'I'm his Hope.' The words just came out. But then she caught herself and announced, 'Detective Sergeant McGrath. John here helped me defend your patient from an attacker. How is he?'

'He'll be all right. We've stopped the blood coming out. Looks like it's lacerated his arm and across his shoulder. We'll take him for some observation. He might be out of action for a while, but he's going to be okay.'

Hope collapsed to her knees, and put an arm towards John, but saw him wince. 'I'm okay, Hope. I'm okay.'

She bent forward and the two of them kissed more out of relief than anything else. As she broke off and stood up, Hope turned and saw the camera team were still there. She turned and walked over, making sure she put her hand on the camera, pushing it out of the way before confronting the presenter.

'Get out,' she said. 'Get out but give me that camera before you do.'

'You've no right to take that.'

'I have every right. That is evidence. You've just filmed a crime. I am confiscating that camera. Give it now.'

The man was only five foot six and Hope dwarfed him, looking down, her red hair straggling out behind her as she'd lost her hair tie in the pursuit.

'Can we just film you like this before you go? I mean, you look the part now.'

'Get out,' said Hope. 'Get out.'

From the corner of her eye, she spotted hospital security and called them over. Two policemen arrived after them, but Hope decided that the better part of valour was to let the security escort the camera crew out, for technically, they hadn't done anything wrong. They'd just known where to be, but she'd let Macleod chase that one.

She turned back, looking at John. He smiled over at her, but he clearly was in a lot of pain. Her hand moved up to the scar on her face, one that had come from defending Macleod's partner, Jane, when she was attacked in their home. Something inside her sunk and a fear gripped her as she looked at John. *How do you take this, Seoras?* she thought. *How do you take it when it happens to them?*

Chapter 12

Macleod looked in through the window at Raigmore hospital. A small cubicle had been set aside for Dennis Gates. The man was asleep and had two police officers standing outside his door. The entire ward had been closed to anyone except visitors or patients, and they were being vetted quite keenly by a constable beside the lift. Macleod had never seen the like of it, an attack on a man coming out of surgery. He made his way down the corridor to see another room where Hope's partner, John, was sitting up in bed looking rather pale and evidently disturbed.

When Macleod had first arrived, Hope had said John had been magnificent, acting in the moment, but Macleod saw someone now struggling to come to terms with the violence he'd experienced. It wasn't an uncommon thing and despite his valour and efforts to maintain someone else's safety, the whole incident was now coming back at him. Hope was standing beside John holding his hand and Macleod thought it quite touching to see her so concerned for someone. Normally she was so aloof, a woman who stood on her own, but the man had got under her skin. *That isn't a bad thing either,* Macleod thought. *She needs someone.*

He stood waiting for Hope but did the decent thing and turned away from the window, allowing them to have their private moment. When a few minutes later, Hope did emerge, Macleod told her to follow him down to the dayroom at the end of the ward where Ross was sitting with his laptop in front of him.

'You're not going to like this,' said Ross.

'Oh, just bring it on,' said Macleod. 'You're going to tell me they've got footage, aren't you?'

'Yes,' said Ross. 'They've got footage, and they've aired it.'

'They're doing it before we even have an injunction, aren't they?'

'Yes,' said Ross.

'I might visit them. I need to find out how. It can't be high profile, though. I can't just charge in. I need to find out how they knew when he was coming out, when the attack would be.'

'Can't you bring them in for that?' said Ross.

'And do what with them? All they'll say is they were coming to film a man who had been attacked earlier. They'd gone up to where he was in surgery and then suddenly, the attack happened, the camera was there, they filmed it. This is what they'll say. But tell me, Ross, how on earth did they get the footage off that camera out of the building?'

Macleod swore that Ross rolled his eyes. 'It's uploaded directly, sir, straight to the cloud. That's how they've done it.'

'Straight to the cloud?'

'Yes, sir. Straight to the cloud. The camera's running, meanwhile in the background, over the Wi-Fi connection, it's sending the footage which is then stored in the cloud, before being accessed by the TV company at their offices. But it's worse than that, sir.'

'What do you mean, Ross?' and Ross spun his laptop round where Macleod could see the *When Justice Fails* logo. It was on YouTube again, but this time it was an update and Macleod watched pictures of the incident.

'Your man was brave, wasn't he?' said Macleod, 'and you didn't half take a beating either.'

'It's just a punch,' said Hope. 'I was a bit woozy after but I'm all right. It'll take more than a punch to put me down.'

'You're not Kirsten. You don't take a kicking for a living.'

Macleod saw Hope flash him an unfavourable glance. It was one thing Macleod had always struggled with, Hope and Kirsten, before Kirsten had left the team and made her way to work for the Special Services. Kirsten was a fighter through and through. She had grown up in an octagon ring, learned mixed martial arts and while Hope may have looked as in-shape as Kirsten and could react quickly, she couldn't take the hammering that Kirsten could. Kirsten was made for it. Hope was just doing her best, which in fairness was a lot better than Macleod ever managed.

'Just wait for the next bit,' said Ross, and Macleod listened as the presenter started commenting on the incident.

'He just said I'm defending a rapist and a killer,' said Hope. 'They're casting me as the bad one in this.'

'Easy,' said Macleod. 'Of course, they are; they're having a go at all of us. They're looking to drive their agenda. Don't take it personally. They won't be giving two thoughts about you. They're just using you because you're there. If they had realised that that's your partner they probably would have thrown him into the mix as well, so let's be thankful for that.'

'Thankful for that, Seoras?' said Hope. 'You must be joking.'

'At least you're not going to have the DCI holding you up as his glamour girl now.'

Macleod was suddenly aware that Ross had spoken out loud but had not meant to. He watched Hope glare over at Ross before Macleod smiled.

'It's true,' he said. 'DCI wanted you as his glamour girl. Maybe they'll all just see a real detective now. I hope so. You deserve to be known as a detective, not some poster image.'

Macleod took out his phone and called the DCI, advising him of what had just happened on the screen.

'I'll get a public statement out. That's ridiculous. Do you want me to speak to the company?'

'No,' said Macleod, 'I don't. I want them to run with it. I want to see where they go with it. These guys are somehow tied-in with this killer. I'd bring them in, but I think they'd just steamroll us and run a heavy-handed police campaign on us. I may visit the station in my own time but if I do, I'll do it discreetly, sir.'

'Seoras,' said the DCI, 'You know I trust you with this, but just be careful. I've been talking with uniform and they're saying there's a bad feeling on the street. A lot of the officers are getting taunted. There are people at times saying we're covering things up, going for the easy conviction. It's all spawning from this programme. It's not the whole city or anything, but there's a certain band of people starting to rise up. It's worrying the Chief Constable greatly.'

'Nothing to worry about from me. I'm always quiet,' said Macleod. 'But if they get in the way I'll go through them, and I won't care about the mess.'

'You never do, Seoras, do you? Anyway, get on with it and find this man in the mask. The sooner we haul him in the better, then get back to normal killers.'

Macleod signed off with a 'yes, sir' and then putting his phone away, he took one look at Hope McGrath and his heart felt for her. 'Are you still good to go?' he asked.

'Of course,' said Hope. 'Always. I don't break that easy.'

'I'm not suggesting you do, I'm just saying, are you good to go? That's John in there. It's not just some punter from the street.'

'I'm good.'

Macleod turned around to Ross, 'Where are we at?'

'Well, Clarissa hasn't got any further. She said she had nothing to share at the moment. We're still working through CCTV trying to identify the car that ran over Dennis. So far, no luck except to note that it was following him out of Inverness, but I can't trace it back to an address yet. It was stolen though, sir. Our killer is making sure nothing comes from him and when he uses it, it's mainly getting burned. Nowak's still back trying to trace the mask. I've got a lot of places that are making them now. People have started asking for them.'

'What?' asked Macleod. 'They're asking for them?'

'It seems so. Looks like he's making a name for himself.'

'Do people actually believe that these people are murderers, and they deserve what's coming to them?'

'You got to see it in context, sir, though, don't you?' said Ross. 'Over the last three months, we've seen various people get off with what seemed like open-and-shut murders. Of course, it wasn't that easy with the evidence, and they weren't all up here in our patch, but the national news gets watched by everybody. So therefore, the common impression is these perceived cases are where the killer got away. On top of that, we've got the TV programme feeding this nonsense, but also not giving out all the facts. A lot of people are getting wound up. They're talking about a march coming.'

'A march?' Macleod hadn't realised how strong the feeling was amongst people, especially as this had all kicked off in the space of four days. 'Okay, Ross,' he said, 'you get yourself back to the station, find me that mask, and where it's coming from. Tell Clarissa I want who's passing these messages out. We've got three bodies so far, and a man fighting for his life and an injured friend, one of our own. I take that very personally.'

'We all do,' said Ross, closing his laptop. He walked over and put a hand on Hope, giving her a kiss on the forehead. He had to stand on tiptoes to do it, and Hope lent forward a bit, but Macleod heard Ross whisper, "You'll be good" before he left.'

'Where are we off to, Seoras? Should we go down to the TV company?'

'No,' said Macleod. 'You're going downstairs for a coffee with me.'

Hope looked at him incredulous. 'I'm good to go.'

'No,' said Macleod. 'We're going down to get a coffee.' When he stood in the lift to make his way down to the ground floor, Macleod could feel the heat of Hope's stare. She was fuming in a way that she did when she really disagreed with him. But frankly, at the moment, Macleod didn't care. The TV company could wait, at least for half an hour. There was something more important to do.

When they got to the coffee shop, Hope went to sit down, but Macleod shook his head, buying her a takeaway coffee to go, and one of his own. He took her outside, never realising that he'd sat her down in the same seat she'd been sitting with her partner not long before.

'What's this? A little pep talk?' asked Hope.

'Stop,' said Macleod. 'Listen to yourself. This is personal. Very personal. They don't teach you how to handle this one because you wouldn't be given a case normally, but John got caught in the crossfire, and that's why you're reacting like this.'

'Like what?' demanded Hope, her shoulders leaping up, her face becoming like thunder.

'Like someone who's trapped in a corner. You need to understand, Hope, you won't make this better for him. This won't go away. You can't magically get a sponge out and wipe away what's happened.'

Hope put her head in her hands. Macleod took her red hair, pulled it into a long ponytail, and then asked if she had any hair ties.

'No,' she said. 'If I had, it would be tied up by now. You know I don't wear it out when I'm on duty.'

'I know,' he said. 'I always think it's a shame, though. I know it gets in your face, but you're one of the fortunate ones. You don't have the greying rubbish I have. You have a mane like a lion, and you don't get to wear it. But you know something, you've got to have a heart like a lion, too,' said Macleod.

'What are you on about, Seoras?'

'You're beginning to feel it, aren't you? The vulnerability. You can't control everything. Normally, work and John are separate. You might take some of work back. You might tell John how you're vulnerable. You might tell John how this hurts and that hurts, and he'll wrap his arms around you and tell you it's all okay.'

'Is that what Jane does for you?'

'Totally. She disassembles me and puts me back together again. She picks at me with her jokes and her humour. She stops me being a prig. She stops me reacting so I'm charging around like God's own avenger. I'm just an inspector. I have a passion for my job, and I want it done right, but that job came at me the day Jane nearly died. The day you saved her, Hope, I died inside. She was suddenly there, suddenly being attacked for something that I'd done because I was the one they were after, and they were going to hurt somebody else to get to me.'

'But John was just here.'

'He was, and he stepped up, and he got hurt for it, and you couldn't defend him. I saw the tape. You were first there, but if it wasn't for John, our witness would be dead. You've got a very brave man there, and you've got to just live with that. You can't protect him. You can't make him not be what he is. He saw you needing help, he saw that man needing help, and he reacted. Jane does the same. She sees me needing help; she knows I need support. She stands with me, and she takes every consequence that comes and because of that, for her, it was almost an acid bath. She never signed up for that.'

'John never signed up for this.'

'No, Hope, he didn't. But, if you weren't there and he saw it going on, would he still have done it? Of course, he would. Just be thankful he's come out the other side.'

Hope leaned over, put her shoulder up against Macleod, then let her head drop onto his shoulder.

'Do you know something, Seoras, if you were twenty years younger, you'd be quite the catch.'

'Don't,' said Macleod. 'You have no idea about my bad side.'

'Oh, I think I do,' said Hope, and Macleod reckoned she did.

'Tell me something, Seoras. How do you do it? How do you live with this constant threat?'

'It's not a constant threat,' said Macleod. 'Also, Jane knows what she's got herself into. She's a big girl. I treat her the same way I treat you. You signed up for this. You know what you've got yourself into. Well, she signed up for me. John up there, signed up for you. He didn't have to intervene. He did it for you. You have to let him be him. You have to let him do what he sees best.'

'But I could have lost him today.'

'And I could have lost Jane. Somebody very dear for me paid the price for saving her.'

Hope lifted her head off his shoulder. Macleod ran a hand up to the scar that went across her face.

'They took away my looks that day,' said Hope, but Macleod kept his hand up.

'No,' he said, 'you never looked more beautiful than you did afterwards. You saved Jane's life but understand if you want him and you want the best for him, you've got to let John be himself. You've got to let him in a little bit. He won't be just a guy sitting at home for you waiting to take on everything that you've had. You've got to be the woman that lets him live, and if that, at the end of the day, means one day we lose them, we lose them, in the same way I might lose you.'

Hope smiled, and then she laid her head back on Macleod's shoulder. 'You know what they call you at the station, don't you?'

'Do I really want to hear this?' Macleod asked.

'Well, it used to be Gramps, because you were that much older than everyone. It's developed into Grumps since then.'

'Why am I not aware of this nickname? Nobody's ever called me it,' said Macleod.

'Of course not,' said Hope; 'they're all too scared of you.'

'Good,' said Macleod, staring across at the car park. 'Good.'

Chapter 13

Macleod made his way out to the car in the Inverness Hospital car park, the snow starting to fall down from a heavy grey sky. As he reached his car, he heard the beep of his phone and pulling it out, he negotiated the lock screen and the password he often forgot. Macleod saw that an email from Jona Nakamura had arrived. Opening it up, he read about an urn found at the roadside near where Dennis and Sheila Gates had died. The ashes inside were found to be those of Kieran Smith, who was convicted of the killing of the boy. He was subsequently run over by the parents of the youth and after he died was cremated. It seemed from initial investigations, the urn had been stolen two days before.

Macleod put his phone back in his pocket, stepped inside the car and found his phone was ringing again.

'Jane, love,' said Macleod, 'I'm quite busy at the moment and haven't really got the time to talk.'

'You need to get to a TV, Seoras.'

'What are they doing now?'

'Apparently there's a special show coming up; it'll be on air in about twenty minutes. If you can get to the station by then, you could watch it.'

'Why would I want to watch it?' he said, annoyed at Jane for even bringing it up.

'Because they're talking about three new cases. That's what they've said. "Dangerous Miscarriages of Justice." Apparently, it's a special show. You need to be careful, Seoras; there's a real growing swell behind this Arbiter of Justice.'

'This what?' said Macleod.

'The Arbiter of Justice. That's what they're calling the person doing these killings.'

'No, no, no,' said Macleod. 'They can't do that. You don't give him a name like that. He's just a killer, he's a murderer.'

'You and I know that,' said Jane, 'but Seoras, that's not what's happening at the moment.'

Macleod slammed his hand down on the steering wheel. 'Okay,' he said. 'Okay, love. Look, I'll be back whenever.'

'Seoras, take it easy. Don't take it personally. You can't deal with everything that's coming here.'

'It's my job to deal with it, Jane. You get that, don't you?'

'You know I get that. Who's been behind you the whole way? Who's stood here and heard you when you've talked about the dark times of this job? Me. I'm as proud as anything of you, but you can't handle everything. You go find the killer. This extra stuff, dump it on someone else. Besides, it's not what you're good at.'

'What you do you mean by that?' asked Macleod.

'Politics, presenting things, showing them in the best light, that's not you. You deal with the truth, you deal with what's happened. Deal with that. Find the killer, find out why he's doing it.'

Macleod closed the call, put the keys in the ignition and drove along the snowy roads the very short distance back to the police station. It was a little bit over the road from the hospital and when he pulled up, he saw Clarissa looking out of the window. She had a rather concerned face on but turned away when she saw him getting out of the car.

Macleod made his way through the station straight to the office of the Murder Team to find Clarissa, Ross, and the new PC, Nowak, watching a television.

'Is that programme coming on?'

'Yes, Seoras. We're watching it for a good reason.'

'I know,' he said. 'I wasn't having a go.' And with that, he plonked himself down on the nearest seat to the television.

'How are your investigations getting on?' he asked Clarissa, his mood indicating he wanted some good news.

'Not well, Seoras. You're asking me to dig deep now. We're up above my pay grade.'

'I know,' said Macleod. 'I also know you won't stop, and you won't hold any airs and graces for anyone up there. I can't be seen to be doing it. I'd attract too much attention. You're always out and about going about things in a rather aggressive way. It won't seem strange to them.'

'Well, I'm not sure how to take that,' said Clarissa. 'What do you think, Als?'

Ross coughed politely. 'Both have your place,' he said just above a quiet whisper. Macleod saw Nowak almost laugh.

'Okay, okay,' said Macleod. 'Let's just see what the TV crew has to say.'

The screen exploded with the logo, *When Justice Fails*. Macleod could see different cut scenes of the previous murders, all taken from distance, but also showing highlights from the YouTube videos that were taken. The actual killings were not shown, but he could see the faces of the victims not long before their demise. The presenter came on, looking sharp and snappy with an assistant beside him who Macleod thought was heading for the catwalk, such was the inappropriateness of her clothing. If she was an investigative reporter, Macleod was the comedian at Butlins.

Between them, the presenters began to talk about three cases, one being that of Kieran Smith, the man who was convicted for raping the boy and shooting him in the case that Dennis and Sheila Gates had been involved in. Two other cases were highlighted. There was mention of Karl Heinz and Sarah Goodley, names Macleod was unfamiliar with.

He nodded over to Ross. 'Find out where they are, what they're doing. We might need to get some police protection for them.'

'If they'll accept it,' said Ross. 'After all, it could highlight where they are.'

'I think if I was them, I'd want some police protection,' said Clarissa. 'This so-called arbiter doesn't seem to be shy about dispatching those he thinks have committed the crime.'

Macleod sat through a piece about how the Arbiter of Justice was pointing out the police cockups. The presenter asked if the arbiter would solve more of these cases, bringing the real killers to the task. Then followed a walk around the streets of Inverness where the public was interviewed, most of whom seemed to be condoning what the Arbiter of Justice was doing. The police took a slating for having been so erroneous in their pursuit of the cases.

Macleod could feel his blood beginning to boil. The arbiter was wrong in some of these cases. He was convinced of it, certainly with Sheila and Dennis Gates. Where did this guy get off making completely unsubstantiated allegations and condoning somebody murdering people who were innocent? Macleod forced himself to sit back to take in what was happening in front of him, try and pick apart the method that was being used to promote these killings, to see if he could find links to the killer. It was easy to get wound up with; after all, that was the whole purpose. Whether to inflame the public or to annoy the police, it was all deflecting away from the key point. In Macleod's mind, that point was a man in a mask was killing people and not following due process to bring them to justice.

Macleod was in complete wonder when another series of interviews seemed to have many of the general public saying that the Arbiter of Justice shouldn't even be investigated, let alone prosecuted. He saw a small band of people with placards chanting and cheering.

'Think we can identify any of those people, Ross? I bet you half of them are from the TV station, or else hired punters. Probably paid for their time. If we could do that, that would—'

'Seoras,' interrupted Clarissa, 'we really should throw that one to the DCI, throw it to public relations. By all means, make the point, give them a handle of how to go about it, if you wish, but that's not our business at the moment. There's deeper things in this than some people who were hired to wave a placard.'

Clarissa was right. Macleod's phone vibrated, and picking it up he saw it was Hope on the other end, and so answered the call.

'It's Macleod.'

'Are you watching this?' said Hope. 'I can't believe it. Did you notice the bit of footage of John in it? They've actually had a go at me and John again.'

'Step back,' said Macleod. 'I'll say it again, just step back. I'm finding it hard to keep my own blood from boiling listening to this nonsense, but we need to. We need to be on top of things.'

'I hope somebody's going to go at them. Get the lawyers. This kind of thing needs blocked, Seoras. This is going to raise a rabble eventually.'

'I'm aware of that,' said Macleod, 'but I'm studying at the moment. Come back to the station. We need to talk about what we're doing because one thing you are right about, this is going to raise a rabble. We need to nip this guy before he gets worse. Who knows how many he's got lined up?'

Macleod put the phone away and continued to watch. After more interviews, and general disgust from the public requesting that something be done where they could support the arbiter, Orla McIntyre came on. Macleod knew the woman from past low-level protests.

'What's she up to?' he said aloud.

'There'll be a march. This is just them getting the rabble up. But you know what Orla's like,' said Ross. 'She'd be up for a protest about toilet seats needing to be green instead of white. Professional activist. Somebody's got her involved, winding her up.'

'There is a higher level of manipulation going on, isn't there?' said Clarissa. 'There's a guy in the middle planning and doing all the murders, but there's somebody else. Maybe it's the TV company.'

'We'll be careful about going there,' said Macleod. 'I'm just aware that they're the ones spinning the story and if we walk in there and get it wrong, they'll spin it back. I did think about going down and seeing them but that will be for the DCI to get to the bottom of it.'

Orla McIntyre advised that the march would be in several days' time, causing Macleod to roll his eyes.

'We need to get on to this quick,' he said. 'Lift this guy before the march. That would take their thunder away.'

'It would do,' said Clarissa, 'but we're nowhere near finding him.'

'Then we better get the head down,' said Macleod. Giving Ross a nod to switch the TV off as the credits rolled, Macleod raised himself from his chair, made his way over to the coffee machine and poured himself a cup before standing, holding it, half-leaning against the sideboard. In truth, he was feeling quite dejected as he didn't seem to be making any progress. The killer was good at covering his tracks and the press seemed to be spinning whatever story they wanted.

Though that was unfair. Most of the press had started off condemning the so-called Arbiter of Justice. Now they were asking when he would stop, if he could be stopped, or, if indeed, was there a point to what he was doing. Even if they abhorred the methods by which he was doing it. Macleod took a sip of his coffee, felt his phone vibrate in his pocket and the ringtone went off. He took it out and saw it was the DCI. Macleod wanted to close down the call but knew that would only bring his boss running down from upstairs. After all, Macleod's car was in the car park and that was the first thing the DCI looked for.

'This is Macleod.'

'Have you seen it?' asked the DCI.

'Yep, I've seen it. Doesn't change anything.'

'The hell it doesn't. This is getting out of hand.'

'With respect, sir,' said Macleod, 'I think this was on you.'

'What do you mean, Macleod? Explain yourself.'

'This is all publicity around it. It's just the TV touting and building it up. You need to put a quash on that. Go to the lawyers, see if you can pull the programmes, see if we can stop this march on a legal basis.'

'The quickest thing to stop all of this is to bring that killer in,' said the DCI.

'I'm well aware of that, sir, but in the meantime all the fires that are breaking out around this case, you could do with putting them out. Run some cover for me.'

'Have you made any progress?'

'Well, we are going forward, I would say that.' But Macleod was not sure how to justify that statement.

'I'll run your cover for you, Macleod, but I want this sorted and I want it sorted before they do this march. God forbid I can't stop it. The thing is I don't think the courts will stop it. We'd have to have a pretty good reason. So far, I can't see it's going to incentivise violence; it's just going be a march and it's going to be all about us getting it wrong.'

'But we haven't got it wrong,' said Macleod. 'Certainly nothing can be proved here that we got it wrong.'

'They don't need to prove it. There just needs to be the doubt and then they build it up. Get me that killer, Macleod. Get me that killer so we can put a stop to all this.' And with that, the phone went down.

Macleod picked up his coffee cup, took a sip, and then put the cup down quite forcibly. Some of the coffee spilt on the counter.

'Seoras?' asked Clarissa from the other side of the room. 'You all right?'

'No,' said Macleod. 'No, I am not. Get me where this information's coming from. Somebody's hanging us out to dry. Somebody's feeding this guy stuff about the cases. Get me it, Clarissa; get me it quick.'

Macleod stormed off into his office and Ross raised his eyebrows across the table from Clarissa.

'Can you blame him?' said Clarissa. 'He's always at peace. It's not like Seoras to drop a bit of coffee anywhere.'

Ross half-grinned, but then his face took on that serious tone that Clarissa had seen before. 'The killer's too well covered up,' said Ross. 'Tracing back, finding out where he's getting his gear and his stickers from, it's bloody hard work.'

'But you could be the breakthrough,' said Clarissa. 'You and Nowak here, stick at it. Once Hope's back, we'll have a meeting, and then I'm going to go and build up my reputation of not giving a toss about rank.'

Chapter 14

Macleod stared at the small hole in the wall of his office. The paint on the wall had been put there three months before during a lapse in the spending control imposed by the facilities manager. Clarissa had been in Macleod's office at the time when a man had arrived, asking what colour they wanted. Macleod had been away for two days and when he came back, Clarissa had organised a light pastel yellow for the walls. Macleod didn't particularly enjoy it, but in truth, it fitted with the carpet on the floor and all his furniture. He had even managed to smile when he saw it, taking away Clarissa's thunder. And to this day, he hadn't let slip just how annoyed he was at her determining the look of his office.

But twenty minutes ago, Macleod had marched into his office, having spilt coffee on the sideboard outside and not mopping it up. He'd come straight through and punched the wall behind his desk. He didn't know why he'd always believed that it was a solid wall all the way along. Macleod had not been party to seeing building construction, but he knew that renovations had taken place to create a space for the murder team within the Inverness Station when they had moved up from Glasgow. They had been used to being travellers up to this area, but now with their new base, they were able to operate on the cases of the north of Scotland.

Macleod looked at the hole again. It had come from his second knuckle alone, and as he looked at his hand, he could see a faint trace of blood. One thing that always bothered Macleod was the things he couldn't control but which were doing immense damage around him. By choice, he'd walk onto several estates known for drugs, family issues, and spousal abuse, and he'd take away the pubs in the centre of them. He'd take away those hang-out shelters built before to try and improve the town, but where people congregated in the evenings, where dealers would stand, dry from the rain, selling their wares quickly before they were moved on by whatever police car that passed. And the first people Macleod would close down were those pointless TV stations.

Macleod was not a friend of the press, but he knew they had a job to do, and if they reported fairly, he never had a problem with them. But these days there were so many conspiracy theorists, so many programmes with such loose evidence that it drove him insane. What really got to him was that Jane watched them and even at times talked to him about them, where he'd have to point out that the evidence wasn't there time and time again. How did such an intelligent woman fall for all this? That he could never understand.

Macleod looked at the wall. In all the time he'd been here, he'd never hit the wall. He clenched his fist. He felt despair, but the sheer anger with which he hit it bothered him, and the anger wasn't at the killer. He was still trying to work out why these killings were taking place. Usually, when someone did something like this, there was a reason in their own life. He was open to the fact that this was a damaged individual, but the TV station that was reporting this, the TV station that was egging everybody up, they were just vultures and they were the reason that Macleod had just smacked the wall.

The door of his office was rapped. Macleod turned to find Hope entering.

'Are you okay?' asked Hope.

'Why shouldn't I be?' asked Macleod.

'Clarissa says you're snapping. That's not like you, not in that way. And now you're staring at the wall and it appears to have a dent in it that it didn't have before.'

Sometimes there was a downside to working amongst detectives. They were sharp with their eyes, and he just gave a grin at Hope. 'Blasted TV in there, whipping it all up, making you and your man out to be the enemy when really you should be being praised. John did a good thing back there. How is he anyway?'

'He's okay. He'll recover,' said Hope, 'but we need to get on.'

'Tell me about it,' said Macleod. 'I had the DCI all over me, but I've asked him to run cover, to go and deal with this march, and the TV station. Well, we need to get on.'

'Are you ready?'

'Of course,' said Macleod. 'Bring them in.' Hope turned around, took her jacket off, and hung it over Macleod's jacket. Then she opened the door and shouted the team through. She turned back, made her way over to the desk that Macleod held his meetings around, and when she sat down, she looked up, seeing Macleod look at her.

'What?' she said quickly, aware that the others would be arriving.

'He's really done you good, hasn't he? In the midst of all this you're the calm one, not me. Who would have thought?'

'They're doing their best to wind me up as well, and they're nearly getting there, but yes, he is doing me good.' Macleod watched Hope smile and inside something felt good. It was hard sometimes to notice the things that were happening around you when the world was becoming a mess, but a little win like this just helped to sustain him through the nonsense that was going on in his work.

When the rest of the team had sat down, Macleod stood up at the desk, looking at them individually, but maintaining silence for a minute.

'Sir?' asked Ross.

'How are we getting on with our tracing of the mask and these T-shirts and stickers?'

'They're all over the place now, sir,' said Ross. 'In fairness to Nowak, she's gone through at least sixty places. I'm starting to think he's done it somewhere very small scale. It might be local, but certainly not on a level where you just order up online.'

'There's no danger he could have actually made them himself?' asked Macleod.

'I doubt it,' said Ross. 'For some of these things, you need reasonably sized machines, certainly to make that mask. Doesn't look hand-done either and he hasn't just made one. He made several.'

'I take it we've asked? We've actually put out a public request?'

'Yes, and we've had lots of responses. That's the problem. Everybody's making these things now. Nowak's been checking through, doing credit card runs. Nobody's coming up on our system as being of note. And that's the problem, sir. We've not got anything here. We can run all the matches we want, we can run across who's bought what, but they have to have done something else to even be of interest. We're missing the angle. We're missing why he's doing this. If we know why he's doing it, we might be able to find out who he is.'

'We've got a problem as well,' said Macleod. 'They've just come on and named two people that they said were the actual killers in cases. Those lives are now at risk. There's always the danger, not just from the killer himself, but from copycats. People get into their heads that they could just arbitrarily exact justice, but it's not justice to exact murder on people. Then we're in trouble.'

'We should take that then,' said Hope. 'Seoras, you and I should look into the protective cover. The rest of the team's busy.'

'I agree,' said Macleod. 'Ross, you and Nowak, you stick on where this stuff is coming from. Hope and I will look into these new allegations and the cases surrounding them.'

'And do you want me to—'

'Yes, I do,' said Macleod quickly, interrupting Clarissa. 'I want you to get all over this force. I want to know where this information is coming from. You don't just pick it up from here and there.'

'I'm getting up into the higher echelons now though,' said Clarissa. 'You were angry before when you slopped the coffee down. I just want to check. How hard do you want me to go at this? We're going to start talking inspectors, DCIs, maybe even—'

'Chief Constable,' said Hope.

'When I keep going up, that's where I'll get to.'

'Extreme prejudice,' said Macleod. 'You go out on this hook, line, and sinker. I don't care who you upset. I'll back you to the hilt because I'll know why you're going to speak to them. And you won't press down too hard on them unless you think there's a possibility. I trust you, Clarissa, and I'll back you up on it. You go out there like there's no tomorrow.'

The woman nodded her head and then sat calmly as several of the rest of the team looked at her.

'The intended march is in just two days,' said Macleod, 'and I don't understand why. Why the need?'

'They could be trying to build up the groundswell of opinion.'

'But is there even a groundswell of opinion, Ross?' asked Macleod. 'Do we think that? Are they just putting what they want on the television, comments that they like?'

'That's done all the time,' said Clarissa. 'Of course, they're driving an agenda, but why?'

'To make TV,' said Ross. 'To make things that people will watch. I heard people are tuning at night to that programme who never have. It's tied in with a real killer. It's tied in with what their name says, *Where Justice Fails.* And people are wondering where the arbiter is going to succeed next.'

'And as I said, that'll be for Hope and me to look after. The rest of you know what you have to do. Two days we have, so shake the tree hard.'

Macleod watched his team rise and make their way out of the office, but Hope lingered, closing the door once the rest of the team had left.

'Why are you so on edge, Seoras?' asked Hope. 'I get what this guy is doing. I get you're annoyed with the TV company, but there's something else, isn't there?'

'You're becoming very perceptive in your old age,' said Macleod, laughing. 'Can you imagine having gone through as many cases as I have?' he said. 'And it's not just me. Plenty of DIs out there. Good sergeants. Even DCIs who've gone through cases. And do you know what it's like when you get to the end of a case? It's not always clean and simple. Sometimes we lose, we don't get the conviction we want. Sometimes when we get a conviction, we know it's what we believe to be true. But all the evidence isn't there, all the evidence was not found. And so, you make a case. It's how our system works.'

'And then twelve people turn round and say yay or nay,' said Hope. 'I do get it.'

'But you're young enough to not be haunted by your cases. There are times when you wonder, *did you get it right*? Then this guy comes along. Can you imagine what he's doing to a lot of our people? Can you imagine how they feel? This hasn't just got the ability to arouse some sort of small rabble, have some protesting, not just the ability to lift up copycat killers and let's hope they don't. The problem here is, Hope, that some of our people will start to second-guess themselves, and not in a good way. They'll be going over and over in their heads. And then when does it become okay to carry out justice on those who've got it wrong? That's the problem with a vigilante. Vigilantes upset the system, but they upset the good parts of the system as well.'

'One thing that does strike me, Seoras,' said Hope. 'Even with all the files he's saying that he's getting hold of, all the information, he seems unable to tell the rights and the wrongs. But part of me wonders, is he getting the right information and selling this story because he needs it? He needs it for his story.'

'You think he's a killer? Or do you think we should be looking at who's been released recently?'

'No,' said Hope. 'Not necessarily him. It could be somebody related to him. He could be making a point.'

'I did get that one,' said Macleod. 'He could be making a point of displaying it in such a way that when it comes to whoever he cares about, it's hard to refuse them being let go.'

'Exactly, Seoras, exactly. We need to get into his background.'

'I know,' said Macleod, 'but the problem is as much as we have punched into that wall, we haven't got anything yet. There's been no leads into him. He's been so good.'

'Yes, he has, very much, but he'll slip up, you wait and see.'

Chapter 15

'Well, that's the full list gone through, Alan. I can't see anywhere that was printing before all this began.'

'Are you getting any hassle from any of the companies? You don't think they've held any of the prints?' said Ross.

'No, Alan, it's all there. Everyone seemed quite keen to assist.'

Ross nodded and made his way round behind PC Nowak, looking at her screen. 'And it's Ross, by the way, nobody calls me Alan.'

'Clarissa calls you Als,' said Nowak.

'Yeah, well, Clarissa's Clarissa, isn't she? For everyone else, it's Ross. From the boss to Hope. I just don't like Alan, I've always been Ross.'

'Okay. You are my boss, after all,' said Nowak.

Ross could feel something churning through his head and he felt he was going to have to leave the comfort of his computer and the warm office and step out into the Inverness snow.

'Andrea, I think it's time you got out of uniform. We need to pay a call on a few places, places that aren't available for online printing. Maybe not advertised so obviously.'

'I pulled them out as well,' she said, 'from the directories. I'll just be a minute so I can get changed.'

Ross nodded and watched his colleague disappear off in her white shirt and black trousers. She'd been a good addition and Ross was very happy with her work. It was nice to converse with someone who understood more about computers than the rest of the team. Clarissa was a bit of a wildcat and in a lot of ways had done a lot more policing than Ross ever had, but when it came to technology she really wasn't that up to speed.

Ross grabbed the car keys and made his way over to the office door, awaiting Andrea's return. He was becoming very fond of his new charge and she had that slight eastern European accent which made him at times think she was out of a Bond movie. One of those femme fatales from the other side of the Curtain, back in the day when Europe was divided.

When PC Nowak returned dressed in jeans and a jumper, Ross thought she looked quite suitable, and he liked the idea that when they went to interview that she could grab the attention of a lot of people. Not just men, but women too, for she was rather engaging.

As they walked towards the car, Ross could see that the woman was nervous, her hands shaking slightly, and she started over a few words. Her English was normally impeccable considering it was her second language. Ross was quite amazed at how well she spoke.

'Just take it easy when we're out here. I'll take the lead, back me up, all we're doing is interviewing people who print things. There shouldn't be any trouble.'

Least I hope there's no trouble, thought Ross. He'd had his fair share of it, especially with Clarissa.

The car journey around Inverness was slow, with the roads covered in snow and everyone taking it that little bit easier.

Ross saw occasional cars had taken a slide into each other, causing a few bumps, and had angry drivers standing beside them. But he was finding no difficulty with the weather, and in some ways seemed to be enjoying himself within the heated confines of the car. When they stopped to get out at their first contact on an industrial estate on the far side of the city, Ross felt the chill through his trousers and wrapped himself up in a large coat. He saw that Andrea Nowak was still in a light jacket that she taken with her.

'Don't you feel the cold?'

'This isn't cold,' she said. 'It's just normal where I grew up.'

There'd been a lot of Polish immigrants come into the city over the previous twenty years, so much so that there was even the occasional Polish shop set up for the food and other items they couldn't get from the normal Scottish supermarkets. And in general, Ross felt they were a great addition to the city. Generally hardworking, with a sense of humour that could match well with the Scottish vibe.

Making their way into the building in front of them, Ross was met by a young woman, who when questioned about what they printed advised that the printing service had long gone and they were now running stationery from the office as a delivery service. Ross turned on his heel and made his way back out.

'Here you go, Andrea. Policing at its finest. You better get used to this sort of thing.'

'The directory said they still were printing.'

'Yes, well, nobody updates directories these days, do they? You just Google everything, see what hours come up. That's the problem. Everybody takes what's on a screen as being for real, it's all accurate. It's only as accurate as what people put in.'

Ross turned and saw Andrea looking at him rather bemusedly.

'Sorry. It's my bugbear. I'm very big on the technology. If it doesn't work, it upsets me.'

'It is what it is,' she said. Ross realised she'd been in Scotland for a while, coming up with such a phrase. The woman looked in her late twenties, and had not reached thirty, with a pleasant feel about her. But Ross noted that when she wanted to do something, she was quite blunt in actioning it, letting nothing stand in her way.

'How're you working the job with the kids?' he said to her.

'Oh, we have care come in. My husband works offshore on a boat. It's not easy, but it won't be a trouble.'

'I wasn't suggesting it would be trouble,' said Ross. 'I just want to make sure I'm able to help you, best I can.'

'You're very considerate,' said Andrea. 'Inspector Macleod, he seems less thoughtful at times.'

'Don't believe it,' said Ross. 'He looks after us; he'll look after you too. It's just when he's on a case, he's quite grumpy. Clarissa pulls him up for it. She's been good since she came on the team. She really gets at him, but the one that changes his mind is Hope.'

'Ah, he likes the pretty girl,' said Andrea.

'I'm sure he does,' said Ross, 'but it's not that. They've been together a while now and they lean on each other more than he'd like to admit.'

Andrea nodded, and as they got back in the car, she offered to take the keys. Ross told her that was fine, but she insisted.

'When Inspector Macleod gets in the car, does he drive?' said Andrea.

'Not generally,' said Ross.

'Because he's the senior officer. You're the senior officer between us.'

'Not really,' said Ross. 'I'm a constable like you.'

'But on the team, you are, so I will drive. Besides, I enjoy it.'

Ross sat back in the passenger seat and realised it felt very strange not being the one in charge of the wheel. It took the best part of the afternoon to follow up on the rest of their leads, and it was when they arrived at the last one that Ross suddenly felt jaded.

'We've had no luck so far,' said Andrea, 'and this looks like another one of these industrial estate places. They're probably just a warehouse.'

'We chase every lead,' said Ross. 'Come on.'

He got out of the car, followed by Andrea. Inside, a man appeared from behind a desk, shouted over at Ross, 'If you want to use any of this stuff, Jim, next door. Okay?'

Andrea went to speak to the man, but Ross put his hand up and shouted back over. 'Okay. That's not a problem.' With that, he stepped through the door and into a reasonably large room, which had a number of photocopiers, large A1 printers, and a machine that seemed to make rubber masks.

'This seems possible,' said Andrea. 'He's got all the equipment that he would need.'

'Go and ask the man what price he charges.' Andrea turned around and walked back out, returning a few minutes later.

'Blimey, he's expensive,' she said. 'Really expensive.'

'Doesn't look like he's that busy either,' said Ross. 'Where would you go? If you were going to make the masks and you couldn't do it yourself, or you wanted these stickers if it wasn't something you could do, where would you go, Andrea?'

'Make sense to go to a quiet place.'

'He's just waved us in here. We don't even have to show him what we're doing.'

Ross called the man through, and he watched as the man limped into the centre of the room with him.

'How can I help you?' he said. 'Do you need help with setting 'em up?'

'No,' said Ross, reached inside his jacket and pulled out his credentials. 'I'm DC Ross. This is PC Nowak. We're investigating the production of certain items in this city, and we need to establish if you could be being used to produce them. I've just got a few questions for you. Have you ever seen this symbol being printed here?' Ross held up a picture of Lady Justice with the red forbidden sign running through.

'Some bloke did that a while back,' he said.

'Do you remember him?'

'Not really. People just come through and go in. I bought this place, managed to get it set up after I had my injury.'

'What happened to you?' asked Ross.

'Industrial injury. I got a heck of a lot of compensation, but I couldn't go back to my old job working out with the refineries, so I decided to set up this print business. I was able to get all these machines, but in truth, I think I'm selling them on soon. I've really just come in here the last few months, something to do. That's the thing at the moment, life's got a bit dull, getting me down. This place hasn't taken off the way it should do.'

'The man that came in here to use your machines, do you remember him?'

'No,' he said. 'I don't generally do. I remember I came in because he was having trouble with the mask. He designed it himself.'

'How does it work?' asked Ross. 'Do they have to bring in a PDF file?'

'You just bring an image, and you then look for a bit of depth. You see, the programme, you can set it in different ways. You can set up one where you've got a flat image. It then makes it 3D for you because you've got to put a face inside it. You press on the system and the system lets you choose what features to pull out more than others, then gives you a rough idea of how it's going to look on the screen with a 3D image. Then you print it and the mask will come out for you. It's quite something, isn't it?'

'It really is quite something,' said Ross. 'Do you know how many masks he printed off?'

'I don't know nothing,' the man said. 'He came in, I barely looked up at him. He went through and he was able to operate most of the stuff. He shouted through a couple of questions, but I didn't go inside. The machines tell me what the cost is. He came through and left cash on the table and went.'

'Did you give him a receipt?'

'No. He didn't ask for one. He was away before I got to see him.'

Ross nearly cursed. They'd finally tracked down where the stuff was coming from and the man here had no idea who his customers were. 'I take it you've put that cash in the bank,' said Ross.

'I have, but I could find out the quantities for you. I'm sure the machines might have a record.'

'If you could, and if you could give me the files that he's put in for that.'

'Will do,' said the man. He hobbled over to some of the machines.

Ross produced a data stick and handed it to him. 'Just stick the files on there.' As the man continued to work, Ross looked around him and Nowak came up to him.

'It's a pretty sad case, really, isn't it?'

'It's a sad case, but it's also someone who could have seen the killer. But he can't even remember. Do you see any CCTV?' asked Ross.

'No,' said Nowak. 'Maybe it'll be outside on the industrial estate.'

'Good idea. Andrea, fan out from here. See if we can pick up any. Go and talk to the companies, see if anybody's got anything outward-facing. I doubt the man's going to have gone on to any other forecourts.'

Nowak departed. It took another ten minutes before the man came back to Ross, handing over the data stick.

'Is your colleague gone?' he said. 'No offense, but she's definitely the better looking.'

'No offense taken,' said Ross out loud when clearly offense was being taken. 'Can you tell me,' asked Ross, 'do you remember the car that he came in?'

The man stood staring around the room for a moment as if trying to recall, but then shook his head. 'No,' he said.

'What was his voice like?'

'Man's voice, really.'

'High, low? Was it deep? Did he stutter?'

'Don't really remember. Man's voice, just.'

'Are you aware at all of what these masks and stickers are being used for?' Ross asked.

'Not really.'

'Have you seen the news recently, or any TV programmes such as *Where Justice Fails*?'

'Don't have a TV. Don't watch it. Read some books occasionally. Generally, just get out, try and keep my head clear. That's the hard bit, keeping my head clear.'

Ross didn't know whether to feel sorry for the man or angry at his complete lack of recall. He thanked him but decided he would put a watch on the small outlet. Making his way back outside, he saw that PC Nowak had already taken the car and so walked along, feeling the cold air cut across him. He picked up his phone and rang into Macleod.

'Sir, it's Ross. We've found where the print's coming from but I'm afraid it's a bit of a dead duck. Owner barely saw him; the guy's quite a down and out. The place is very run down, probably going to be bust soon. I've got some files brought to see where they've come from on a computer, but it's a bit of a long shot. Not sure what else we can do with it. I've got Nowak going round asking for CCTV from the industrial estate it's on. But honestly, at the moment, we're coming up blank.'

'Blast it, Ross, I was hoping you would get a break-through. Good work anyway.'

'I'm going to set up a watch on the place just in case he comes back. Because if he does, I doubt the owner's going to do anything. Man seems slightly spaced out.'

'Good idea,' said Macleod, 'And let's hope he does because we need a break.'

Ross ended the call and then stood with his thumb out as he saw the police car coming towards him. He got inside and saw that Nowak had turned the heating system over to cool.

'Just 'cause you get to drive doesn't mean you get in charge of the heating system,' said Ross and flicked it back round.

'I thought you said we were equal,' said Andrea.

'I did, didn't I?' said Ross, and he turned the heating system back to the very middle. With that, Andrea gave a smile at him.

'But you, when we get back to the station are hunting through this data stick to see if you can find where any of the files came from.'

Andrea turned and looked at him sourly. 'And I was beginning to like you,' she said.

Chapter 16

Clarissa pulled out her notebook, flipped over the page, and ticked another name. The woman she'd just spoken to was about four inches taller and had glared daggers at Clarissa. The conversation had started smoothly enough until the particular DCI in question realised Clarissa might be implying something. There was then a thunderous exchange about why Clarissa was checking up on people, and wasn't that a job for anti-corruption? The last she'd heard of Clarissa, she was on the murder squad after coming through from working in the art world.

Clarissa had been undeterred and had calmly explained that this particular chief inspector had had her paws on several files regarding murder cases over the last number of years. At first, the woman had told Clarissa to get out, told her that Macleod could come himself. But when Clarissa said that Macleod would be more than happy to do that, and, in fact, she had his blessing, the woman's face had changed. The tension was still in the room but information about why this particular chief inspector had looked at those cases was forthcoming.

Clarissa was now making her way through to Records to touch base on a few items that had been mentioned, and to clarify that they were taken out at the right time in regard to other cases the chief inspector was working on.

Clarissa was smiling because actually, she liked the woman, and she understood her well. She ran a tight department, took no nonsense, and the very idea that she would be involved in anything like passing out details to murderers on the outside was beyond the pale. If anyone would have come after Macleod suggesting this, Clarissa would have been the one to jump to his defence, never mind he to his own.

Sitting in the Records Department, Clarissa checked through the last few details and ticked the female DCI off her list. The list was getting shorter, but it had started with over twenty people, and that was just the ones outside of her own department. Macleod had said to start there, for he was happy with everyone within his own group. And certainly, Clarissa wouldn't want to be the one seen as betraying Macleod. He'd tear apart anyone that did that.

After checking through the last few pieces of paperwork to satisfy her about the female DCI, Clarissa made her way to the canteen, sat down with a cup of coffee and a small biscuit, giving herself five minutes before she started on the next task. The trouble with having to investigate those higher up and without the mandate that would come from an internal investigation was that Clarissa was constantly sliding in, trying to make contact before then asking very awkward questions.

Police officers, being police officers, realised when they were being questioned in such a way that alluded to the fact that they may have been passing out information. Most, quite rightly, especially those who were innocent, took great offence at this, the very nerve of it, but Clarissa and her team were merely following the evidence. So, the one thing she wasn't was rattled when she got a negative reaction.

Clarissa ate the last piece of the biscuit in front of her, licking her lips of the sugar, and was about to stand up when a hand was pinned on her shoulder.

'I think you want to sit down for a moment, don't you, Sergeant?'

Clarissa recognised the voice. She'd seen the man many a time, a superintendent operating out of Inverness Station. Within the entire building, he was the one who said what happened and was ultimately Macleod's boss. Superintendent Gordon Black had risen up the ranks and made a name for himself on the uniform side of the force. He was quite the person with outside stakeholders and had a great working relationship with the press.

In some ways he was the exact opposite of Macleod, and within the force, a lot of people had felt that he was quite washy when it came to investigating crime. Most of his work had been done on initiatives and schemes rather than the day-to-day police detecting. However, he was also a large man, six foot four, shoulders like a large trunk tree had fallen on its side and a chin that was square set. As Clarissa watched, the man kept his hand on her shoulder before sitting down beside her, one of his deputies joining them at the table.

'What are you at?' asked the chief constable.

'Excuse me, Gordon,' said Clarissa. Now that everyone was on first name terms due to an edict put out the previous year, Clarissa made sure she used it with a lot of senior officers.

'Sergeant, talk has been coming my way. I've been told you're hunting someone within the station. Don't you think the least you could do is come to me with that?'

'I'm doing my job,' said Clarissa. 'I've been tasked to look into who touched certain case files because the details of them seem to be going for a walkabout to our murderer outside.'

'And so what, you thought you'd do a little bit of freelancing inside, turn something up to show Macleod?'

'No,' said Clarissa, picking up her coffee, drinking it slowly before putting it back down and licking her lips. Only then did she look back at Gordon Black. 'Seoras is more than aware of what I'm doing. In fact, he ordered me to it.'

'You seem to be enjoying it. I've had complaints.'

'Complaints?' queried Clarissa. 'I have been the very model of patience, understanding, and tactfulness.'

'I'm not sure you know the words, but I'll tell you this, stop causing a ruckus. We need the station to function. I can't have my inspectors knocked asunder because of some wild allegations.'

'Wild?' asked Clarissa. 'How do you know they're wild? Have you been looking into this too?'

'Don't you mess me about,' said the man, his fist thumping down on the table, so much so that the rest of the canteen looked round.

'I am messing no one about,' said Clarissa. 'And I'll thank you not to thump the table like that. You nearly spilled the coffee.'

'Don't you give me coffee,' said Gordon Black. 'I'm warning you; you're pushing this too far.'

'This is intimidation,' said Clarissa.

'It's not intimidation, it's a clear instruction for you to back off.'

'No,' said Clarissa. She picked up the remainder of her bun, the last few crumbs that had fallen on the plate, wiped her finger around that plate, picking them up, and then putting them in her mouth before chewing slowly. Then she answered.

'This is intimidation. The reason it's intimidation is you're on the list. I need to check why you had these files.'

'I don't need to answer to you. You're so insolent,' said Gordon Black.

'Was that a refusal to cooperate? I'll make sure Seoras hears that one.' Clarissa fixed her stare, daring the man to come back with something but instead, he thumped the table again, this time with his left hand.

'Don't you dare. Don't you dare. I've been too many years in this uniform. You show some damn respect.'

'I'm not allowed to show respect,' said Clarissa. 'We're investigating several murders. We're investigating collusion; therefore, there's no respect. There are just the facts. All I do is work off the facts, and the facts say that you touched a number of these files. In fact, if I have a look—' She pulled out her notepad, flicking through it again. 'Yes. You touched every single one of them.'

'Of course, I did. Always looking at case files. I run the damn station, woman. What do you expect?'

Clarissa smiled inside to herself. She'd got him. She got him answering her question, albeit a denial, albeit a good reason why he had these files. Previously, he'd simply been attacking her. Now he answered questions.

'I don't see why you need to have all of them,' said Clarissa. 'Awful lot of coincidental files. What other files have you been looking at?'

'I'm not telling you what I'm looking at.'

'I think you should. I can see if this as a consistent pattern. I'd imagine if you're looking after the whole station, what you're going to do is have a certain amount from each area of different files, so the files that have been picked up of murders and that should be roughly equal to those when we're talking about theft or drugs or any of the other sections. That's fair, isn't it?' Clarissa stared at the man and saw him grunt.

'Keep your nose out. You're nearly as bad as your DCI. Finally get some press. Finally get somebody taking an interest in the cases we're running and all we do is complain at them. You need to seize it. Tell Macleod he needs to seize the moment. Go to the press, start talking about the stories.'

'Excuse me! I think the last thing we need to do is talk to anyone, especially the press. So far, they've been spinning inaccuracies left, right, and centre.' Clarissa could feel herself becoming somewhat heated. She reached out to take the scarf off her neck, folding it gently as she spoke. 'The important thing to remember is not to give the press too much.'

'Nonsense,' said Black. 'You control the press. You control these TV stations.'

'You do that very well, don't you.' said Clarissa.

'What's that meant to mean?'

'They always said to me that you climbed up the outside of the building. You didn't take the hard stairs through the middle. Rather you popped outside and climbed up the easier set.'

'Watch yourself. You're on very thin ice, Sergeant.'

Clarissa looked down at her notebook. 'Maybe, but yours is looking thinner. I'm noting this down as a hostile act from a witness.'

'Don't you even dare,' said Black. 'This is not how you're going to find your killer, running around through the station, dragging up issues of the past. You need to get out there, be more visible.'

'Would there be a particular time that I could ring you, or

would you like me to pop up to the office?' said Clarissa. 'It's just with what you've told me today, I would like a little bit more time to look into why you had a lot of these files.'

The canteen was silent. Even the kitchen staff had stopped, and Clarissa watched Gordon Black rise, pushing himself up with his fist. 'Just don't push it, Urquhart. You're not long in here. I can send you packing.'

'Still aggressive,' said Clarissa, writing in her book. Then she closed the book shut and looked up at the man. 'I don't take to threats well, I don't take them at all. You don't come after me, and if you go after Macleod, I'll bury you.'

'Who do you think you are?'

'I'm Clarissa, Clarissa Urquhart and I may not be the tidiest, primmest, or best-looking sergeant in this place, but I'll scrap like none other. You better not be dirty, Black.'

'I'll do you for slander. I'll kick you back down. God help me, I will destroy you. That's the trouble, Macleod bringing in these trumped-up little clowns. I see you near me, I'm bringing him in. I've had enough of this.' With that, Black thumped the table and began to walk off.

'Is that a no on the interview then?' asked Clarissa. The man continued to walk but only when he went through the door did he hold up his hand, the back of which showed two fingers in a V shape.

Clarissa looked around, saw the rest of the canteen staring at her. She stood up, made her way over to the serving hatch and asked for another cup of coffee. She made her way back to the table with it and clung to it desperately, forcing her hands not to shake. All eyes were on her but she was giving nobody the satisfaction of knowing that Gordon Black had actually shaken her inside. She sat for five minutes, slowly drinking the coffee, then stood up and walked out over to the ladies' toilets. Once inside, she pulled out her phone and called Macleod.

'You okay?' he said. 'You sound quite shaken.'

'Seoras, I've just had a toe to toe with Black.'

'Superintendent Black?' said Macleod.

'The very same. He came after me because I was kicking up a fuss. I called him out in a polite way, but he doesn't want to see me, doesn't want me to meet him for me to ask questions. He's had his hands in every file that's gone out. He's a potential suspect.'

'What did he say to you?'

'Well, apart from the fact he would break me, he'd also come after you as well for bringing these trumped-up little people in.'

'But are you okay?' asked Macleod. 'Do you want me to send Hope down, or should I come myself?'

'No. Just give me a moment,' said Clarissa. 'I'm in the ladies,' I'm just taking a breather.' She talked away, some tears coming down from her eyes. When the man had thumped the desk, she'd almost jumped out of her skin.

'The one thing I'm sure of, though, Seoras, is he's got something to do with it.'

'Well, if he has, I'll go for him,' said Macleod. 'You know that, don't you?'

'I do,' she said, 'but to be honest, I think he's going to be coming for us first.'

Chapter 17

There was a knock at Macleod's office door, and he looked up to see what until fairly recently, was an unfamiliar sight. Normally, he could tell who was at the door through the glass. Hope was six feet tall, one of the few women in the station of such a stature and easily identifiable. Clarissa would be there in some type of bright-coloured arrangement and Ross's knock was so formal that you could identify it from a mile away. Jona Nakamura was diminutive and had a light knock that seemed to carry an immense amount of gravity for how weak it sounded but this knock was more of a rap-pa-ta-tat with the door then half swinging open and a head popping out around it.

'Ross said it would be okay, said you needed this information.'

Macleod looked over at the new PC on the team, Nowak, and thought hard to remember her name. 'Alison, come in.'

'It's, er, Andrea, Inspector.'

'And mine's Seoras. Not a lot of people use it round here. You can say boss if you want, but if you want to use Seoras, it's okay. Sorry I haven't been about very much to say hello to you and welcome you to the team.'

'Yes, we kind of hit the ground running, didn't we? One of those situations but I'm trying to be very useful with Ross.'

The woman's English was good if a little stuttering at times but when Macleod lived in Glasgow he'd heard less clear English, and most of that was from the locals.

'What have you got for me?' asked Macleod, leaning back in his chair. Andrea entered the room, made her way forward, and put a couple of sheets of paper on Macleod's desk.

'This is a report. Apparently, there's been a lot of incidents recently. Some of the activists have been getting edgy, I think Ross put it, with the police. Been a few minor arrests and a couple of scuffles with uniform.'

'I can feel it,' said Macleod. 'Can you feel it? Things are very tense at the moment. It's ramping up. We need to get to the bottom of this, Andrea. We need to sort out who's causing this.'

'You think someone is behind the scenes, someone other than the murderer?'

'Yes,' said Macleod, appreciative of where the woman's thoughts were going. 'Do you see it as well? It's like there's a conductor on board.'

'Like in a band?'

'Exactly. Somebody pulling the strings, winding everyone up. For what reason, I don't know. There's some other purpose here. I'm just about to go out and call on Karl Heinz, one of the alleged killers the TV programme talked about.'

'Why are they allowed to make such accusation?' asked Andrea. 'I didn't think you could.'

'They're very clever, aren't they? They never actually say it, they just put out evidence that sort of leans towards—they insinuate.'

'You mean they say it, but they don't say it?'

'Exactly.'

'And one other thing,' said Andrea, still standing almost to attention in front of the desk. 'Ross said that Dennis Gates was attacked on leaving hospital.'

'Was he? How badly?' asked Macleod.

'They didn't have to take him back in,' said Andrea, and Macleod thought he saw a faint smile.

'No, but how badly?' asked Macleod.

'A few scrapes and bruises but he's gone on home.'

'No,' said Macleod, 'this is not wise. Tell Ross to organise the safe house. He needs to be put away somewhere safe for his protection until we solve this. Tell Ross to get on it.'

'Okay, Inspector.'

The woman turned to walk away, but Macleod shouted her back. 'Look, Andrea,' he said carefully, 'my apologies. I got your name wrong; you'll find that I'm not good on that side of things, but Ross said you were impressive so I'm looking forward to you being here. If things occur to you, you say them. You speak. Do you understand?'

'Yes, Inspector. I understand.'

'You need to be aware, Andrea, Ross is polite about everybody but he doesn't sing many people's praises. He thinks you're the bee's knees.'

'The what?'

'The top dog, the best.' Macleod saw the woman smile and even redden a little in the cheeks. 'Work hard, do well; you might even get into the squad proper one day, not just doing the numbers. Maybe transfer over to be a detective.'

'Thank you, Inspector,' she said and made her way back out of the office leaving Macleod wondering if he'd managed that initial meeting well.

Macleod picked up his phone and gave a call to Hope. She was out in Inverness. 'Have you found her yet?' he asked.

He was referring to Sandra Goodly who had been pointed out as one of the alleged killers.

'No, she's not at her home address. Looks like she's gone to ground. I'm chasing up on the rest of the family, but no one seems to know where she is. Either that or they're hiding her.'

'Well, keep on it. Dennis Gates got attacked on leaving hospital, I'm off to Karl Heinz. We need to make sure this goes no further, Hope. With the march coming up, attention in the city is getting crazy. Ross pointed out there's been a large number of scuffles between police and protesters. I just wish we could put all these activists back in their cage. Stick them in the house for a couple of days.'

'A free country, sir; that's the way it is.'

'Indeed, it is. How's John?'

'He's still a little shaken but he's doing okay. He might even make it back to work tomorrow.'

'Tell him to take it easy. No point going back to work if he's not ready.'

'Yes, you're talking to the boss there, Seoras. He runs the place. It's his firm. You're not going to keep him away. And also, when did you ever keep away from work because you weren't well?'

'I never said I was an example to follow. I just dispense wise advice.'

Hope laughed. 'Go and see Heinz. Tell me when you get him,' said Hope. 'I'll keep chasing Goodly.'

Macleod closed down the call and made his way out to the car. He wondered if he should take someone with him but thought, given the circumstances, he'd best go alone. Hope was busy. Ross had his work to do, and Clarissa was having a hard time with the upper echelons of the station. Besides, maybe a solo policeman would seem a little less intimidating to a man who had just been put up on a TV screen as being an alleged killer.

Macleod had two addresses for Karl Heinz, an old one and a new one. The first, the old one, was nearer to the station and so he called to find a young couple living there. They confirmed that Karl had sold them the house and he now was elsewhere, so Macleod got back in his car and made his way to the next address.

This was a semi-detached old-style house and Macleod thought it looked rather neat. The garden was immaculate, a row of planted geraniums about the only flower that Macleod could identify. He made his way to the front door, and rapped it to find that the door swung open. Once inside, he took a look at what appeared to be a messed-up living room.

The chairs were all sitting as they should be, nothing was turned over, except that there were a number of magazines lying around as if they'd simply been thrown. Macleod saw a cup and looked down into it to see a pool of coffee. He took his finger, placed it inside the cup, and found that the coffee while not being blisteringly hot, was still lukewarm. His heart quickened. *Had somebody come in here already?*

He moved quickly through to the kitchen but again found no one but did note that there were dishes on the drainer. Making his way upstairs, Macleod found a bed and the covers had been thrown back. The place had been lived in and recently, but once again, there was no one about. Macleod made his way downstairs, looked out, and saw a car in the driveway.

He pondered for a moment, then made his way into the hall and looked where the coat rack was. He pulled the coats away and saw a small door at the bottom about half a person high. It would be the cubbyhole where you would store maybe the hoover, shoes, or whatever. Macleod tapped at the door gently.

'This is Detective Inspector Seoras Macleod. I'm not here to do you any harm, Karl. I'm here for your welfare. If you're hiding in there, would you please come out and speak to me; there's no one here.'

There was silence and Macleod reiterated his message. When he got no response, he gently tapped on the door forcing it to open and took out his pen torch pointing it inside. There was a man deep within the cupboard pushed back as far as he could against the walls. Macleod looked at the face and recognised him from the prepared sheets about the case he'd had on his desk.

'Karl, you need to come out. I need to talk to you.'

The man was slow to emerge, and Macleod made sure he blocked off the exit to the front door. The last thing he needed was the man running so he wouldn't know where he was.

The man stood up, looked at Macleod and Macleod was suddenly aware that the man only had Macleod's word that he was indeed a detective inspector. He pulled his credentials from his pocket, handed them over to the man who gazed at them for a good solid minute before handing them back. 'Mr. Heinz, you obviously are in a situation.'

'A situation, Inspector?' the man blurted out. 'Why are they doing this? Why is my face on TV saying I'm a killer? I'm not a killer. I wasn't anywhere near the place. Back then, they tried to pin it on me.'

'Who?'

'Other people. The people who were supporting the man who went down, Danby. Danby's people. They came around to the house at the time, goading me, trying to get all my neighbours against me. Now, it's happening again. Look, the TV, why is my face on the TV? I went next door before I realised. They didn't want to know me. The woman on the other side, she pulled her kids away from me. They all think I'm a killer now because of that bloody TV programme.'

Macleod didn't know what to say because ultimately, it was true, so he decided to focus on something slightly different. 'You said they went after you back then; what did they try to do? Was there anything more than just simply coming around and causing noise?'

'Oh, there was evidence. Evidence of this, evidence of that. One of your people.'

'One of my people? Who was it?'

'He wasn't like you. He had a uniform, but he was quite high up. I remember people looking at him, your people, other policemen, and all they said was, 'Yes, sir,' to everything. He tried to say there was evidence against me, pulled me in time and time again.'

'But it was a murder investigation. Surely the detectives would have been doing that?'

'No, he had a uniform, and did it several times.'

'But Danby's still in jail from my records,' said Macleod.

'And they want to keep him there. The man is a murderer.'

'Well, you went to court, sir. You went to court, and they said you were innocent. They convicted Danby.'

'But it didn't stop after that,' said Heinz, 'and now they're coming again. This time it's coming through the TV. I have to move again.'

'I can put you in protection,' said Macleod. 'In fact, I'm suggesting that you do this. Protection will keep you safe until we get to the bottom of what's going on. We have a lunatic out there killing people he thinks were guilty but given as innocent. I would say that makes you a target.'

'I don't want protection,' said Heinz. 'I'll go on the run. I'll hide. I can hide better than you can hide me. Forgive me, Detective Inspector, you may be one of the good people, but after the last time, I don't want the police involved with me. I'll keep clear.'

'Do you remember the name of this uniformed officer, the one who kept taking you in for questioning?'

'Black. It was always Black.'

Macleod nodded and handed over a card. 'If you get into trouble, Mr. Heinz, or if you need us, or if you have had second thoughts and think, "I want to go into protection," you ring me. Don't ring the station, ring me. I will protect you. I will put you somewhere where only my team know.'

The man's eyes went narrow. 'But how do I know I can trust you? I've got nothing to base that on,' said the man.

'True,' said Macleod, 'absolutely true. I could tell you to phone the station, tell you to find out what I'm like, if I'm trustworthy, and they'll tell you I am, but that won't convince you. There's nothing I can really put forward if you've had a bad experience before, but if you need me, I'll be there to protect you.'

The man took the card and placed it in an outside pocket of the shirt he was wearing. 'Thank you, Inspector,' he said, 'but you'll understand if I can't go through with what you want.'

'Perfectly,' said Macleod, 'just be aware. What will you do now?'

'I'll be gone from this address after today,' he said. 'I'll hide where people can't find me.'

Macleod couldn't force the man to do anything. After all, he was innocent and the one who was being attacked. Macleod thought about getting someone round to look at the forensics of the scene but in truth, it would probably be pointless. This looked like the rabble, people causing distress to the man, and in truth, not of that bad a level, for most of the home was still intact. Macleod got into his car and drove back to the station. He made his way into his office, sat down, and began to pour through the case file regarding Jeff Danby once more.

There was a tap on the door and a head popped around again, but Macleod didn't speak and simply waved PC Nowak inside. She placed a coffee on his desk and retreated without a word.

'Thank you,' said Macleod without looking up. His eyes were scanning through the case file over and over again. He found where it was noted that evidence was allegedly tampered with, but it was evidence that was muddying the water, evidence that was trying to point towards Karl Heinz. When he read through the rest of the evidence, it seemed to him that Jeff Danby was definitely the killer.

Macleod sat back, taking his cup in his hand, and drank the coffee slowly. Black, Superintendent Gordon Black. Clarissa had had a run-in with him. Macleod thought things were beginning to shape up. *Danby, maybe he was the key for it all, but why? Why would Black be defending Danby? Why would he look to try and put the blame on someone else?*

He'd stepped across the line. Black had certainly moved in and trodden over the murder team's patch. Maybe he was just uniform helping out, but he clearly couldn't help out enough to convince them that Karl Heinz was the killer. *Black, Danby, and the blasted TV*, thought Macleod, *what's the connection?*

Chapter 18

Hope raised her arms to the sky, stretching out her back as much as she could before twisting at her hips, taking her arms all the way down to her toes. She felt the muscles in the back of her leg stretch hard, and then she rose, letting them release. She was in and out of the car all day, feeling a little bit under strain between running the case and checking up that John was all right. Everything was feeling like that it was a little bit too much.

She had spent most of the day looking for Sandra Goodly, the woman who had been mentioned as an alleged killer in a case that had not been dealt with correctly by the police. The case file had certainly seemed to indicate that Sandra Goodly wasn't responsible for the death of a child, but with the hubbub that was being drummed up by the television, Hope was finding it difficult even for her to push away any images they were showing.

Sandra Goodly, however, seemed to have gone to ground. Hope turned up at her house to find protesters outside, but there was no one in. When she spoke to a neighbour, she said the woman hadn't been there for a week. Hope found out where the woman went, checked at her local gym, checked her workplace, but no one had seen her for a week. Concern had grown for the woman, and Hope had a bad feeling about where she was. It was that detective nose, that instinct, the one that unfortunately proved to be too often right. Hope's was not as sharp as Macleod's, and she almost thought about ringing Seoras to ask him what he thought about the situation, but in truth, Hope knew something was up.

She was walking along the side of the canal to a spot that Sandra Goodly was reportedly interested in. One of the staff where Sandra Goodly worked had indicated that during lunchtimes, Sandra liked to take her packed lunch and sit down on the bench, watching the canal. The woman had even been able to pick out Sandra's favourite bench. Hope had made her way there only to find a man with a large coat, several bags, and a dog sitting on it. Hope made her way over and sat down beside him.

'I don't want to alarm you, sir, and I'm not trying to move you on. My name is Detective Sergeant Hope McGrath.'

The man looked at her. 'I can't see you would alarm anyone,' he said. 'Do you know how many women walk past here? Most of them are like the men,' he said. Hope was beginning to get a distinct smell off the man and wondered when he'd last washed. 'They don't look my way. Quite frankly, you could be whoever you want to be. You can even be here to move me on,' he said. 'It's just nice when you get a little bit of contact.'

Hope eyed the man up, wondering if he was having a laugh at her expense, but he seemed quite genuine. He put his hand out towards Hope. 'Would you mind?' he said. 'Just shake it. I don't want anything funny. Just shake it.'

Hope put her hand forward and shook the hand. The man's grip was not tight but rather gentle. They continued the handshake for about twenty seconds before Hope eventually retracted her hand.

'Thank you,' he said. 'First person to have touched me in a week.'

Hope was feeling bad. All she wanted to do was ask the man what she needed to know and then get out of there.

'Is there a woman that comes to this bench quite often?' asked Hope. 'I mean, if you're in the area a lot.'

The man pointed over across the canal towards the hedge on the far side.

'Don't tell anyone but if you go through there, you'll see there's like a little low-level shack I've set up. I managed to find some scrap corrugated iron and put it over the top. Got some sides, some plastic that was able to keep the place warm. It's where I sleep.'

Hope was horrified.

'Can't you go to one of the shelters?'

'I don't want to,' said the man. 'I really don't want to.'

Hope wanted to tell him that he needed to, that obviously his life was going wrong, but part of her remembered the conversation she'd had in the station talking about people on the streets. The officer in question that told her not to judge them, not to decide why they were there or what they needed to do. He said you had to listen. Hope didn't want to listen because the situation seemed awkward to her. She felt a bad person for that, but she convinced herself that the work needed to be done.

'Sorry,' she said, 'but I need to ask you, is there a woman that comes here. Do you know of her?'

'I see most people about here,' he said, 'but you haven't even asked.'

'Asked what?'

'My name. If you're going to ask me about a woman, you're going to need my name. Name and address, isn't it? You can put it down in your book.'

'Of course,' said Hope. 'Who are you?'

'Jockie,' said the man. 'Jockie Wilson.' Hope made a note of the name in her book then looked up to see the man laughing.

'What's up?'

'I played darts as well,' he said. 'Look at the rolling belly on me,' and he laughed loudly.

Hope had no idea what he was on about. 'Look, Mr. Wilson, I need to know, does this woman come here often?' Hope pulled the photograph from inside her jacket pocket, showing it to the man purporting to be Jockie Wilson.

'All the time,' he said. 'Well, during the week. She's not here on the weekends. She sits here with her lunch, quite nice actually. She says hello to me when she goes past. Hasn't shaken my hand though. She looks less uncomfortable than you do but maybe she's just seen me more often.'

'When was the last time you saw her here?' asked Hope.

'Whoa,' said the man. 'I mean, every day seems the same, but it must have been at least a week. Yes,' he said. 'At least a week. Have you lost her?'

'She could be in trouble,' said Hope and then felt her phone vibrating in her pocket. Her ringtone joined in and she took out the device and saw a message from Ross. It had a link to a YouTube clip and the expression, *One minute ago*. Hope clicked on the link and when the video started to play, she saw the same face that she had just shown the homeless man opposite her. She found Jockie standing up, making his way over and looking over her shoulder.

'That's her,' he said. 'That's the woman, isn't it?'

'Yes,' said Hope. The volume now kicked in and she heard Sandra Goodly confessing to killing a child. There was plenty horrific about it, but Hope's detective mind kicked in. She listened to the detail being given, or rather the over-detail. There was a lot of information about a child suffering, a lot of emotion about how she felt about killing a child, but there was no detail on how it was carried out. Hope was sitting thinking about all the questions in an interview room she would ask to prove if this was genuine, because at the moment, there seemed to be a lot of holes in the statement.

Sandra Goodly said that she strangled a child and watched as the life drained from the kid, and suddenly a face peered beside her. It was the face of Lady Justice with the forbidden sign. The man in the mask had turned up again. Announcing himself as the Arbiter of Justice, he slipped a rope around Sarah Goodly and Hope fought to continue watching as he strangled the life from the woman.

'Dear God,' said Jockie. 'What on earth?'

'Sorry you had to see that,' said Hope. She was continuing to listen to the Arbiter of Justice as he spoke, announcing another victory for the forces of justice. He then gave an address that he was at, committing this crime.

Hope rang Ross. 'I'm only three or four minutes away,' she said. 'I'll get there quick. Get hold of Seoras.'

'He's out and about,' said Ross. 'Been trying to get hold of him.'

'Okay, well, I'll make my way,' said Hope.

'Be aware,' said Ross. 'This thing's gone crazy on social media, there could be a lot of people there. I've asked uniform to get plenty of people down.'

'On my way,' said Hope, standing up from the bench, beginning to run.

'Nice to meet you,' said the man. 'I hope she'll be all right.'

The man had just watched her die on screen, thought Hope. *How on earth was she going to be all right?*

She didn't look back, now that the guilt about the homeless man was washed away by the need to do a job. Hope got into her car, negotiated the roads for five minutes and pulled up outside a detached house. She could see a crowd already there and noted that there were three police officers blocking the entrance, carefully forming a semi-circle around the front door. Hope got out and strode towards them, putting her credentials in the air, waving them around for everyone.

'I am Detective Sergeant Hope McGrath; you will all step back away from this property.'

'Like hell. We need to get her. We need to get her.'

'No, you don't,' said Hope. 'You need to get back. There is a crime scene inside; you will not go in and ruin it. Step back.'

Someone tried to force their way through and the young police officer at the front door pushed him back. The man trying to get in then threw a punch, catching the officer on the jaw to loud cheers around him. Hope reached over, grabbed the assailant's arm, drew it up behind his back, forcing a cry from the man. She then took him to the street before depositing him there.

'You step back inside the grounds of this house, and you'll be arrested, sir. You've just assaulted a police officer.'

Hope turned and saw more people pressing in at the door. She ran back, again pushing through the crowd to the front door, shouting at them to stay back. The officer that had been punched had got back up, but blood was flowing from his mouth. Beside him was a small Asian woman who had drawn her night stick, urging the crowd to stay back.

'Stay tight,' said Hope. 'Stay tight together. Help is on its way,' she said under her breath to her colleagues around her.

Hope realised she was the tallest of the officers there and looking over the crowd, she could see more people arriving. In the distance was the wail of sirens. *Thank God,* she thought. *They're coming. They're coming.*

But then the crowd in front of her pushed again, trying to get into the front door. She watched the group break, making for the rear door of the property and she shouted at two of the officers to follow through the house and secure that door. Maybe Hope should step inside and shut the door properly.

She edged back, pulling her Asian colleague with her. Drawing her inside, Hope ran in and tried quickly to close the door, but several legs and feet were instead forced into the gap and Hope was pushed back. She bent down, drove her shoulder into the person who had just come through, pushing hard.

She felt someone grab her hair, pulling her ponytail round and Hope raised her hand up, grabbing somebody's face, driving their jaw upwards. She heard them cry out and the hand was released from her ponytail, but not before they had taken off the tie and her hair started to spray around her.

'Push,' she shouted to the Asian colleague beside her, and the small woman bent down, driving her shoulder forward. There were now only two people trying to get through the door at this time but the mob behind them was trying to press in as well. Hope could feel the power of the mass, heard those at front begin to shout out in pain as they got crushed between Hope and the pack behind. Hope's legs were buckling, and she knew pretty soon they would just pile through the door.

Then the pressure was released. She could hear cries from outside, people being manhandled away and as the people in front of her were suddenly flung and dragged out through the garden to the street outside, Hope looked up and saw two vanloads of police officers. Hope paused, waiting to see that everyone had been pushed back away from the house.

There was now a cordon, and several people had been arrested and thrown in the back of two vans. More police vans were arriving as well as other cars and Hope realised that the scene was becoming calmer and secured. Chanting began outside the ring of police officers, demanding to see Sandra Goodly, but Hope told the officers to man their posts and not let anyone through.

She stayed inside the house and thought about what she'd seen on the video, making her way upstairs because she thought she'd seen a bed in the background of the video. She opened the door, being careful not to touch it with her bare hands.

It was the main bedroom. Inside, she saw a photograph of Sandra Goodly on the wall, but on the floor lay the body of the woman. Hope reached down, but she could find no pulse, no sign of life at all. Regardless, she called for an ambulance because you never knew. She turned her over and began to do CPR on her.

Hope continued but found no sign of life until the ambulance crew arrived. It took them only a couple of minutes to advise that she was definitely deceased. Hope was reeling. She'd been involved in the struggle, then she'd found the dead body, and she'd worked hard. Sitting on the floor of the bedroom, she drew in large draughts of air to keep her going. It was then her eyes glanced up and saw the wall.

There was a large poster, recently stuck up by the looks of it. There was the face of Lady Justice, the red ring around it with the forbidden sign. *No way do the TV cameras get to see this,* thought Hope.

Chapter 19

Clarissa was livid. She'd been called out and chastised in the middle of the canteen, and as much as she felt she'd given a robust defence, she was not happy at what had occurred. Macleod had backed to the hilt, but she was determined that she would find more than circumstantial evidence of the deputy chief constable having scanned the various records around the murders that had occurred previously. It would take a lot more than that to prove he had been handing over information to the television company or indeed, to find out exactly how he was involved in the proceedings. Clearly, he had something to lose due to the heavy-handed manner in which he had dealt with her.

Clarissa was en route to the records department in the basement of Inverness Police Station, a place where what she thought of as the computer geeks lived. They looked after systems, controlled the network. She believed that these folks could best enable her to discover the truth of what the superintendent was up to.

Clarissa had only been down once and expected, at that time, to see a rather dingy office, all screens in the blackness of a room but in fact, it had been incredibly bright. Every computer station she went to had a number of work items around the screen whether there was a cover in front of it to enlarge the screen, a special mouse or keyboard, but she was absolutely bemused at the hardware in front of her. She managed to ask one of the *geeks* about the software being used and after two minutes, had tuned out completely. Clarissa didn't see herself as an unintelligent person, but when it came to computers, they had arrived a little bit after her and certainly, she hadn't much dealings with them when she'd been chasing antiques.

Clarissa descended the last stair and opened the door to the records room. In days of yore, you would have had numerous files everywhere but not anymore. Everything was either in the cloud, as she thought they called it, or in some large storage facility. So many terabytes, as the man had described it. Clarissa had asked about what size of building was required to hold that and had got a rather bizarre look. The man showed a box giving some number and Clarissa just did not believe that you could store that many records in a box that size.

Pushing the door open, Clarissa set foot inside and found herself beginning to shake a little. Up until now, she had asked some probing questions, but this was on the other side. She was going for the jugular. Her intuition knew that Superintendent Gordon Black was involved but now she was going to have to prove it, or at least, to come up with a line of inquiry so further investigations could take place. She was going to have to come at it from a slightly funny angle.

Clarissa stepped into the room and picked out who she thought looked like the person most capable of handling technology. This observation was based on the size of his glasses, his dress sense, and how much paraphernalia was around his computer. Of course, these were all arbitrary factors, but Clarissa felt she had to have some sort of technique in picking out the right person to help her in her search.

'Hello, I'm Sergeant Clarissa Urquhart and I need any one of you to give me a hand.'

'If you want to write the request down, we can get on to it, add it to the pile.'

'Actually, I need to talk to you in confidence about something,' said Clarissa.

'Okay, if you want to come through into the other room with me.' The rather lanky man stood up and Clarissa peered upwards. His legs seem to stride even though he was walking casually. Clarissa fought hard to keep up before they entered the other room.

'Well, what is it I can help you with?' asked the man, turning around to look at Clarissa while sitting on the edge of a table. The room was sparse, and Clarissa struggled to see any technology in. 'Ah,' said the man, 'here's where we like to eat if we don't want to be too far from the computers. We don't tend to eat in there.'

Clarissa nodded, as if what the man had said was revolutionary, but she raised herself up to her full height before dropping the word she hoped would get hold of the man's attention.

'DI Macleod would like some work.'

'DI Macleod, the detective inspector?' said the man, stuttering slightly.

'That's correct,' said Clarissa, 'and he's asking that you keep it under the radar.'

'Well, I can't not record what I'm doing.'

'Of course not,' said Clarissa, 'he's just asking that you don't talk about it, especially with your colleagues.'

'Okay, but if he's looking for personal records, I can't do

that.'

'No, he's not wanting that,' said Clarissa, 'what he wants to know is all of our files relating to murders in the Inverness area, he's looking to see which stations are looking at them the most, and by stations, I mean computer stations.'

'Just so I follow,' said the man, 'you want me to work out where the files have been accessed from, so that you can work out which of the computer stations is being used the most. Why?'

'Well, some of the information on those systems is quite confidential, we just want to be aware of where that information is being passed around. I'm not entirely sure myself, but the inspector requested it.'

'Well, the inspector could simply fill in a form.'

'Like I said, Detective Inspector Macleod wants to keep this under the radar. He said to me to get it done. He was quite blunt, and he wasn't too keen about anybody standing in his way. I recommended you guys would be good for it, discreet but also very, very competent. He likes discreet and competent people.'

'Well, I'm sure we can do that,' said the man, 'if he fills in a form, I can get back to him in a couple of weeks. We've got quite a lot on.' Clarissa stepped forward, positioning herself in the face of the young man. She looked up and smiled, her hand going up taking her scarf and adjusting it, flinging it out behind her neck.

'The inspector has asked me to get this done this afternoon. I'm sorry to take you out of your way but if we get a refusal, he might come down here himself.'

'Detective Inspector Macleod will come down here?'

'Yes,' said Clarissa, 'he doesn't like to; he keeps out of people's way, but if people get in the way, if he feels they're obstructing what he's trying to do, he's not behind the door in making sure that people are aware of who did that. He's not behind the door in making sure that their bosses understand how obstructive people were.'

The man nodded. 'Let's see what I can do for you, okay? I take it, you want this to be a private inquiry so rather than go back to my desk, let's go to one of the booths over on the far side of the main office. We can do things a little bit quieter over there.'

Clarissa smiled and let the man lead his way across. Once he had sat down and began logging into the computer, Clarissa leaned over the shoulder of the man, two hands resting on the chair but touching his shoulders. She wanted to make sure he was aware that he was being watched very closely. She hadn't a clue about most of what he was doing but as long as he realised that somebody was watching.

'When you say murder cases in the Inverness area, how far out do you want to go?'

'Thirty or forty, let's say thirty miles. That should keep us within the Inverness catchment.'

'Okay,' said the man, and Clarissa watched him enter search terms. 'Does it have to be murders?' he asked.

'Absolutely. Definitely murders and with a conviction, not open cases—with a conviction only.'

'Okay,' said the man, 'we can do that. So, the first thing to do,' he said, 'is to find out which of the files apply so I'll do a quick search.' The man leaned back and tilted his head back to look up at Clarissa smiling, 'This won't be long.' There was a trumpet sound coming from the computer, which the man almost laughed at and then he had pointed to the screen,

'That's the cases in front of you there. Seventy-five I've got, stretching quite far back. How recent do you want them to be?'

'The last ten years.'

'Well, now we're down to under forty.'

'Now, what I want you to do,' said Clarissa, 'is to tell me who has accessed those files?'

'Who?' queried the man. 'I'm not sure I'm allowed to do that.'

'Sorry,' said Clarissa, 'I wasn't clear. I want to know which terminals have accessed it.'

'Okay,' said the man, 'it's pretty irregular but if Inspector Macleod has asked for it.'

'He has indeed. Like I say, he's trying to see where eyes are looking at our documents. He's a little bit worried that a few places might be insecure.'

'Of course, that's understood but we're not saying who has accessed them,' said the man, 'I'm not giving you any names of who have accessed those files. I need a special request for that.'

'Of course,' said Clarissa, 'of course.' She watched the man type in some more variables and run a search again. A list of numbers came up in front of her.

'What's that?' she asked.

'That's the addresses where the files were accessed from, the computer stations.'

'It would be more helpful to us if you could say where they are.'

'Okay,' said the man, 'I'll just generate a quick table for you.' Two minutes later, he was sitting with a print-out in front of Clarissa, pointing at different numbers. 'This one here,' he said, 'is the murder investigation team. This one is, that could be your desk, in fact, a number of computers in there.'

'Just run me through the top numbers,' said Clarissa.

'I am doing,' said the man, 'The bulk of them there are in the murder investigation team's office. That's Inspector Macleod's office, that's your office; all of those ones. There's only one other towards the top of the list that isn't in your office.'

'Who's that?'

'That's the secretary for the Superintendent.'

Clarissa nearly cheered but instead, she stood holding her bearing, 'That computer has been used to look at how many of these files?'

'Phwoar, 95% of them,' said the man, 'certainly, over the last six months to a year. In fact, if . . . just give me a minute,' he said. He tapped in some more variables. 'Over the last year, that station has been used more than any other.'

'Right,' said Clarissa, 'where is that station exactly, just so, you know, we can be aware if it's an unsafe location?'

'It's in the secretary's office. If you go upstairs,' said the man, 'to the top, as I understand it, the secretary sits outside. You'd have to knock to go into there, and the office of the superintendent is beyond that. There's other waiting areas, but the secretary has her own private space, but it's got a window to look out for others arriving.'

'It's quite secluded then, so it should be pretty safe. You could be reading this without anybody really knowing what you're looking at it?'

'Well, I guess so,' he said, 'the secretary may be there. She wouldn't look out of place.'

*Neither would the Superintenden*t, thought Clarissa. 'Do we have times of access?' she asked.

'I can get them if it's really necessary, but it is a fairly safe location.'

'Well, you're best doing it because the Inspector, sometimes, he just comes out with these questions, he expects us to have thought of them already. Obviously, time is an important factor, some things are more secure sometimes than others. It's just best if I cover my bases,' said Clarissa, shrugging her shoulders as if nothing was important. Inside, her heart was pounding.

'Okay,' said the man, and he did another printout before handing it to Clarissa.

She looked at the times, the majority of them were outside the hours of nine to five. 'Thank you very much,' said Clarissa. 'Thank you very much, indeed.' Then, she put her hand out to shake, indicating the man should tell her his name.

'Kevin,' he said, 'I hope I've been able to do enough for you.'

'Oh, this is excellent, Kevin, thank you very much,' said Clarissa. 'I'll make sure that Inspector Macleod knows how helpful you've been. Make sure he's also aware that you've been working with us on this. Like I say, he wants to keep everything very hush-hush. He doesn't want people alarmed that there may be somebody looking at things they shouldn't.'

'Well, is there?' asked Kevin.

'Well, so far, you've proved that there isn't,' said Clarissa, 'so that's good. Thank you for your help, and remember, mum's the word.' The man nodded. 'Like, I say, I'll make sure Inspector Macleod knows you've helped.'

Clarissa turned on her heel and marched out of the doors to the steps that led upstairs. Inside, her heart was singing. She had found what she wanted, and now she was going to get into her car and drive to a certain secretary. It was dark outside, as she approached her car, and as she clambered into the little green number, someone stepped out of the shadows towards her.

'I hope you haven't forgotten our conversation.' Superintendent Gordon Black stared at Clarissa, his hands clenched tight.

'I'm well aware of what you said.' Inside, Clarissa's heart pounded, for, on the seat beside her, was the paper copy of all the details she'd just received from Kevin.

'Just make sure you understand; Macleod too, or I'll come for you,' he said.

'Then you'll have to see me down at the theatre, that's where I'm off now, can't be late,' with that, Clarissa started the car and drove off, her heart thumping. She didn't look back and forced herself not to race, trying to be as normal as possible.

The trip took her to a block of flats near the water at the centre of Inverness. The town was alive, and she could see some of the activists walking around with placards. Clarissa strode in her long boots, large bustling skirt, up the steps of a block of flats, pressing the button on the door of one of the top accommodations.

'Can I help you?' asked a woman as she opened the door.

'I'm hoping you can,' said Clarissa, and showed the woman her credentials. 'I'm sorry to bother you, but we have a security issue within the station. May I come inside?'

The woman opened the door and Clarissa made her way inside. There was a table with a plate, a knife and fork, and a large steak, glass of red wine was there too. Clarissa looked around but saw no one else. 'Dining alone?' she said. 'Good, I don't mean to keep you from your tea; you can eat away if you want.'

The woman looked at her, lifting her hand up to the cross

that hung around her neck, twiddling it.

'You don't have anything to fear,' said Clarissa, 'but we feel that some of your equipment may have been being used without your knowledge.'

The woman looked incensed. 'How do you mean? I close it off every night.'

'Oh, I'm sure you do. Can you just confirm to me that yours is one of the computers that isn't open for everyone to use?'

'That's correct.'

'Just confirm for me,' said Clarissa, 'that your name is Deborah Williams, Secretary to the Superintendent.'

'That's correct,' she said, 'what is this about?'

'We believe that your computer is being used to access certain files and I'd like you to look at the following times.'

Clarissa held up sheet of paper, showing the login times of access to the files.

'I'm not in for most of this, you can ask anyone, I disappear at five-thirty at the latest. Nearly all of these are six o'clock and beyond. Some of them are nearly the middle of the night. I'm in at nine, never earlier.'

'There's two in the middle of the day though,' said Clarissa, 'would you have been around then?'

'It's possible, I do go for lunch around then. Just a second, let me have a look.' The woman disappeared off to her handbag and brought out a small diary. She flicked through and then she called Clarissa over. 'Look, those two dates,' she said, 'that one, I was at the dentist, over that time you can see; I've written it down in my diary. The other one I'm off sick.'

'Okay,' said Clarissa, 'thank you. Just to make you aware, the Superintendent knows what we're doing and I'd ask you not to speak to him about it or to mention it at all within the station or to anyone else. You've done nothing wrong, and you've been very helpful. We'll be in touch on another date.

'How serious is this?' the woman asked.

'Very,' said Clarissa. 'You may be required to testify, but as I said, the powers at the top are aware of it, so please don't pass it on to anyone. Don't even speak about it in the office.'

'If I must, of course, I'll stay stum. Who do I get in touch with if I see anything else unusual?'

Clarissa gave Deborah her mobile number but not her card. 'Alison Mobley, Anti-Corruption. You may see me about the place. If you do, don't look at me. Don't make eye contact. Just treat me like a normal person you don't know.'

'Okay. I have seen you about before, though.'

'It's been a while, but I'm operating undercover, so please, mum's the word.' Clarissa smiled, looked over at the woman's food, 'That steak looks good,' she said. 'I'll let you get on and eat it. Must get some dinner of my own.' Clarissa made her way to the stairs, let the woman close the door. About halfway down, she gave a little skip, her fist to the air. *Damn well got you, Black,* she said to herself, *I damn well got you.*

Chapter 20

Macleod had arrived at the scene of Sandra Goodly's killing and as the night began to go dark, he stood with Jona Nakamura while her team searched for any type of forensic evidence. Macleod knew that Clarissa Urquhart was on to something and had dispatched her to find out more, but he also needed to hunt down the other side of what was going on. His visit to Karl Heinz had made him wary of leaving it too long and with the march due inside another day, Macleod was fearful the whole thing could just blow out of proportion. Macleod's mobile went off. He shook his head as he saw it was the DCI on the other end of the line.

'This is Macleod.'

'We need to get on top of this. We need to put out a press statement before that TV show gets involved again. I'm going to come down, Seoras. You and I can make a statement in front of the house. It's important we make sure that you're front and centre with me, show what we've got a handle on the case.'

'I thought you'd be better dealing with the media side, with all due respect, Chief Inspector.'

'Seoras, you can't run away from it all. I need you there.

You're the poster boy, you're the one they all know. You're the one who's bagged the criminals before. Like it or not, your name is something in this town, so I need you there. I'll be down in about twenty minutes and then I'll talk through how we're going to play it.'

Macleod switched off the phone and felt like throwing it across the room. He didn't need this now.

'Something wrong, Seoras?' It was Hope from the far side of the room watching him carefully.

'DCI wants to do a press conference. Wants me here. He called me a poster boy.'

'Well,' said Hope, 'you do look the part and you've got the results in the past.'

'You'd look better, Hope,' said Macleod. 'You know I don't do the face of the station that well.'

'He's not wanting somebody who looks good on the screen. He's wanting someone who the public know has got to the bottom of things. Your name's trusted. These people have had their trust in the police shaken. That's why the DCI wants you up here. Don't have a go at him for doing the job you asked him to do, Seoras.'

Macleod shook his head. 'I know you're right, but I really don't need it now. We need to move. When I saw Karl Heinz, he was scared. This is the case that's important. Karl Heinz, Jeff Danby. The march is going ahead tomorrow. The only thing that hasn't been resolved, the only case from that blasted programme is the Jeff Danby one. Something is in the back of the Jeff Danby case. Jeff Danby, the Superintendent,' said Macleod quietly. 'Something to do with a TV. We need to find out. We need to go and get hold of Jeff Danby's family.'

'I've been looking into it,' said Hope. 'He's got a mother on a council estate in Nairn. I was going to go over there with you and see what we can dig up.'

'Well, you're on your own,' said Macleod. 'I've got to go and reassure the public. Head now, don't leave it to the morning. We need answers.' Hope nodded and made her way out of the house, leaving Macleod looking around.

'Inspector, I've got this covered if you want to disappear,' said Jona. 'If it's anything like previous scenes, I doubt there'll be much to find, but we'll do what we can. I'll be contacting Ross about that poster to see if it came from that shop.'

'Good, Jona,' said Macleod, but continued to stand looking around the room.

'I've got it,' said Jona. 'I'll let you know if anything comes up.'

'Sorry,' said Macleod. 'I've got to wait for the DCI. We're going on the telly in about an hour. I need to reassure the public.'

'Why don't you go and sit somewhere and think,' suggested Jona, 'because that's what you're doing at the moment; you're standing somewhere thinking and your very presence here is putting all my people on edge.'

'Why?'

'You really don't know just how fearful people are of you at times, do you? "This is Macleod; he doesn't accept any less. He wants the best and he wants it now." Give you your due, Seoras,' said Jona, coming closer and whispering. 'You're good with people. If they do the work for you, if they get there, you do give them praise, you push them up, like you have done with Hope. But you're very demanding. People that don't know you think they have to make it work. So, do me a favour; go and sit down somewhere else and think.'

It wasn't many people who could speak to Macleod like

that, but Jona was a trusted friend and sometime meditation partner, one of the wisest people Macleod knew. Despite her younger years, Macleod reckoned she displayed more knowledge, compassion, and understanding than many of the older colleagues around him.

'Will do, Jona, will do.'

Macleod made his way down the stairs and walked around to the back of the house. He didn't want to go to the front because of the cameras, but at the rear of the house he stood and watched the trees in the back garden. Part of him wanted to be with Hope because that's where the case was going to unravel. He knew it, but he was stuck here. *Go get them, Hope,* he thought. *Go get them.*

* * *

Hope had driven all the way to Nairn without stopping, her hands occasionally drumming on the steering wheel. She knew she was carrying Seoras' hopes. He had been keen to come, but he had to do what the lead investigator had to do, and as his deputy, Hope was determined not to let him down.

When she arrived in Nairn, she ended up in a street she didn't recognise. Having lived up and around Inverness now for a while, she had visited many of the outlying places, Nairn being one of them. Yet she'd never been in this particular part of it. The streets were fairly run down, everywhere seemingly needing a good coat of paint. There were occasional boarded-up houses, and Hope watched the occasional disgruntled kid kicking about the place. A man walked down the street, clearly drunk, and when Hope parked up, he made his way over towards her.

'All right, gorgeous? How's about you and me?'

'If you really want to date a policewoman, you give it a go, sunshine,' said Hope. 'Otherwise, on you go.'

'Ooh, feisty,' he said. 'I love a feisty one.' Then he caught Hope's look. 'Don't mean anything by it, love, don't mean anything by it. On my way.'

Hope chuckled to herself; It was funny the type of drunk she got. There were those who were more comedic, but it was the violent ones that really struck her. They were hard to handle. This guy just seemed like a happy old soul having had two cans too many.

Hope made her way up to a door that should have had a pane of glass set in it. Unfortunately, the glass was gone, and a wooden board covered it. There was no knocker, no doorbell, and Hope banged loudly on the door.

'Who the hell is that? If that's you again, Tommo, I'm coming for you.' The door opened and an older woman of maybe sixty stood facing Hope. She was in a dressing gown which lay open, revealing some nightwear underneath. Her hair was a casual mess, and her eyes were bloodshot, mascara blotched around them.

'Who the hell are you?'

Hope pulled out her credentials, holding them up beside her. 'Detective Sergeant Hope McGrath. Are you Janice Danby?'

'I was. I am now Janice Shooter.'

'You remarried?' said Hope.

'No, I just changed my name. When your son goes to prison for murder, especially the murder of a kid, you change your name, don't you, love?'

'Can I come in?'

'Why? What the hell do you want with me?' demanded the

woman. Hope could smell alcohol and the woman looked slightly unsteady.

'I want to talk to you about your son. I can do it nice and loudly here on the doorstep or we can talk in there. We don't want the neighbours finding out, do we?'

'Get your arse in then, love,' she said. 'Bloody nasty one, you.'

Hope stepped inside the house and could smell the damp. 'Roof's leaking,' said the woman and pointed Hope through to her living room that consisted of a brown leather sofa with many a patch ripped off it. Sitting in a chair in front of a coal fire was a man dressed in his pants and a vest. Hope looked at him, but the man was flat out, snoring away.

'Don't mind him. He won't be up for hours. In fact, he'll probably sleep till the morning. He's had a couple of pills as well as the booze. Looks like I'm out of luck tonight.'

If that was luck, thought Hope, *I would want to see it turning against me every single time.* Instead, Hope pointed to the sofa, allowing the woman to sit down before she joined her on the other end of it.

'I'm investigating some connections with your son, Jeff Danby. I take it he is your son?'

'He's one of my sons,' said the woman. 'Jeff and Owen, but Owen's gone. Owen sodded off ages ago.'

'What was that about? Why'd he leave?' asked Hope.

'When Jeff got convicted, Owen said Jeff was innocent. Owen worshiped his brother. Jeff was five years older, and Owen always looked up to him. Jeff looked after him but then Jeff got put away. Owen wouldn't have it. I told him to leave it, I told him Jeff was bad. He'd always been bad to me.'

'And what, Owen left?'

'Yes, just went off.'

'Did he go to his father?' asked Hope.

'Father? What father?' she asked, looking around the place.

'Who's his father?' asked Hope. 'That's all I'm asking; didn't he go to his father?'

The woman stood up and Hope could see the tears starting. 'I don't even know who his father is. Back then I sort of hung a bit with a couple of people, got into a bit of a bad crowd in some ways. Had to do the odd little thing for people,' she said.

Hope needed to clarify as the woman didn't seem to be making much sense. 'When you say did for people, did you entertain men?'

'Entertain, love? That's a really nice word. That really is nice.' The woman lurched about and made her way over to pick up a bottle of whiskey that was sitting on the mantelpiece. She opened it and took a large slug from it.

'I entertained two men at the same time. Two friends; one was a policeman and the other one was in filming or something, TV. They were good to me, for a price,' she said. 'I was on the harder stuff back then, not this,' she said, holding the whiskey bottle in front of Hope. 'I wasn't on this. I stuffed it up my nose back then. They could get me it all and for that they stayed with me, and I *entertained* them.'

'So, one of them is Owen's father?'

'Yes, and one of them is Jeff's father. I don't know which is which, if one of them is both or if there's different ones for each. I don't know, they just looked after me back then.'

'I take it they don't look after you anymore?'

'Bastards,' said the woman. 'Just left me, but that's when I started to rebuild. It's when I got this place.' The woman looked around. 'Was good before it got a bad roof. Do you live somewhere with a bad roof?' slurred the woman.

'My roof is fine,' said Hope. 'But tell me more about these men. What were their names?'

'Dan and Jim, but that's not what their real names were. They never told me their real names, just Dan and Jim.'

'You were with them for how long then?'

'Six, seven years,' said the woman. 'And then they just dumped me. I think I got old. I think I must have got ugly. I could still *entertain* so I must have got ugly.'

Hope was feeling sorry for the woman, and she watched her double over, tears now flowing.

'Do you have any images of them, photographs?'

'They didn't let me take photographs,' said the woman. 'No, they said just, 'No photographs. You want the nice magic stuff, you don't get photographs. But I have one. They're a lot younger than they are now, but I do have one.'

'Could you get me it? I'd really appreciate it,' said Hope. 'I don't have to take it.'

'Okay, love,' she said, and the woman staggered out of the room. She came back two minutes later, while the man in the seat continued to snore. 'There you go. This is my time with them,' said the woman, and slapped the album down between her and Hope. She opened the cover and Hope almost turned away from the images she was seeing. The woman clearly had *entertained* them, and every image in the book was of the woman. 'I was prettier to men back then,' she said. 'Prettier.'

'Can you just show me the photograph of the men, please?' said Hope.

The woman flipped through quickly. 'Little bit jealous of how I look, eh?' said the woman.

'Something like that,' said Hope, keen to avert her gaze until the woman came up with the correct photo. When she did,

Hope saw an image of two men on a bed fast asleep. The photo, fortunately, was from their shoulders to the top of their heads.

'Have you got one of your son, of Owen, please?' asked Hope.

'Do you want one of Jeff as well?' said the woman, and then she almost fell over and staggered as she thought. 'Well, you've got one of him, haven't you? You'll have taken one when they put him away. Take it he's still in the lock up. Hasn't been to visit his mom. Neither has Owen. Tossers.'

The woman made her way over to the mantelpiece, picked up a couple of photographs that were lying face down, handed them to Hope. 'Jeff and Owen, that's them.' The woman took the whiskey bottle and sat down again and began to drink some more.

'There you go, love. That's my sodden life. Look at that over there in that seat. Waste of ruddy space. If he didn't pay the bills, he wouldn't be here. Fat, he is. Fat.'

With that, her head rolled back. A minute later, Hope watched the whiskey bottle fall onto the sofa and the woman became limp as she fell asleep. Hope picked up the photograph of the two sons, and with her phone took an image of the other photograph of the two fathers.

Hope stared at one of the men in the photograph. Certainly, it looked like someone she knew, but she couldn't be sure. But at least Seoras would have something now. She had done what he wanted them to do, she'd got the story and the detail. Somebody on TV, somebody on the force and a brother looking to vindicate his older sibling. Suddenly everything was coming together.

Chapter 21

DC Ross looked at the photograph in front of him that had been sent by his boss Hope McGrath. It was of a young man in his thirties and Ross pondered the eyes. The eyes were the windows to the soul, according to the Bible, and Ross wondered if that was how Macleod did it. He sized people up in an instant. Ross sometimes wondered if he knew they'd committed the crime before he'd even worked out how.

The photo was one of two men, neither of whom Ross recognised, but the photograph was from some time ago, Hope describing it as the two men who Janice, Jeff Danby's mother, had been with. The younger man was Owen Danby, her other son. On receiving the photograph, Ross had made his way directly right to the print shop but had found it to be closed. At last, he had something he could show the man in there.

Ross had sent word back to the station and PC Nowak had sent through several addresses procured from council records for people with a similar name to that of the owner of the print shop. Ross made his way to two houses and could have told himself they weren't the right ones by the sheer look of the place. Everything was immaculate. A car in the driveway, children upstairs working in their rooms, efficient wife or indeed husband arriving at the door. His third visit was to a barge sitting on the Caledonian Canal. As he approached, he saw a man on deck and recognised the proprietor of the print shop immediately.

'Hello there, I'm back again.'

'Oh, it's you,' said the man. 'I've just got to lock up for the night. Get down below, watch a bit of television or something. I can't go back and open up the shop.'

'I'm not looking for the shop to be opened, sir, I just need you to look at a photograph for me.'

That seemed to pique the man's interest and he walked off the boat to the canal side, making his way towards Ross. The night was dark and so Ross's phone shone brightly with the photograph.

'Do you recognise this person?'

'As I said, I barely saw him when he came in more from outside, but yes, that could be the person we were talking about. Definite possibility.'

'Just a possibility?' queried Ross. 'You can't be a hundred percent sure?'

'No, I can't. Like I said, I never really saw the man well, but it certainly fits. Sorry, I'd like to be of more use, but you did ask if I can say for definite and I can't.'

'Fair enough,' said Ross.

'Now you've shown me the photograph, he was in a week or two before as well. He paid cash. He always paid cash, that guy. I didn't even see him half the time. He left it on the desk on his way out, like I say. Sorry, Officer.'

Ross noted and thanked the man before making his way back to his car. He had hoped that photograph would bring up a new lead somewhere to go, but as Hope had said they didn't know where Owen Danby was. PC Newark had started looking through addresses, but he was nowhere to be found on any register.

Ross made his way back to the station, and on entering found his boss in the office pestering Nowak.

'Can we check through any photographs, scan the CCTV around the area, see if that person comes up?'

Ross made his way over. 'Can I help you, sir?' he said politely, placing himself in between Nowak and Macleod.

'The inspector was asking about going through the CCTV. I said that would take a while, trying to see if we can find the man in the photograph at any of the crime scenes.'

'Of course, sir, we can do that,' said Ross. 'But not PC Nowak, she'll be going home now. I'll get a couple of the other uniforms to get on to it.'

'Okay,' said Macleod. 'Soon as. Hope was, and I'm pretty convinced too, that this is a lead we need to follow through. We also need to identify the two men in the photograph.'

Ross nodded, before taking Macleod to one side. 'In the future, sir, can you run all requests through me, even if you have to phone me? It's just that Nowak has a family and other issues at home. She can't be like we are on the murder squad. She's a resource for it, she's not a full member of the team.'

Macleod wanted to react, and Ross saw him almost say something in the heat of the moment, but the man retracted and nodded. 'Of course, she's part of your group,' said Macleod. 'Of course, I will.' The inspector walked back to his office, dissatisfied but having done what Ross considered to be the right thing.

On reaching his office, Macleod sat down behind his desk,

not knowing what to do with his hands, his thumbs twiddling, and his eyes watching a picture on his desk of two men from a long time ago. *What sort of person would be in the police force now who used a woman like that*? he thought. *Had connections to drugs*. It was all very unsavoury.

Macleod couldn't recognise the man at all from his younger form. These days he'd be older. If he'd worked hard, he'd be somewhere at the higher level of the tree. Or maybe he'd even been busted back down; maybe he was still operating on the lower levels and that's why Macleod couldn't think of him.

There was a rap at the door, and Clarissa opened it, looking rather glum. 'Tomorrow, then,' she said. 'That's when the march is, and we still have nothing to go on.'

'I was going to wait for Hope to come back,' said Macleod. 'But let's not. Grab your coat. I'm going to take you to meet someone I wouldn't call an old friend, maybe more of a colleague.'

'Not even a partner?' queried Clarissa. 'A colleague? So, I take it you two didn't get on?'

'Not in the slightest,' said Macleod, 'but of course, that was him. He couldn't get on with anybody.'

'Of course, it was all his fault,' said Clarissa. 'Clearly, I mean, how could anyone not get on with yourself?' Macleod raised his eyebrows, and Clarissa backed down. Macleod saw the cheeky grin on the side of her face.

'Well, life hasn't treated him too well,' said Macleod. 'Last I heard, he was in a nursing home, ready to end his days. That's the trouble, you see, he enjoyed too many things.'

'Heaven forbid we enjoy things,' said Clarissa.

'Not the good things. Not the good things, Sergeant. Go on, grab your coat. Let's go.'

'Shall we take my car?' asked Clarissa.

'If you must,' said Macleod, standing up and making his way over to get his large coat and hat. 'I take it you still like to drive with the top down in this weather?'

'I'll make an exception for you,' said Clarissa. 'You have to do that for the older folk.'

Before Macleod could check the comment, Clarissa was away and as Macleod looked back across the room, he saw Ross's shoulders on the move but when the man looked up his face was perfectly straight.

'I'm on the phone if you need us,' said Macleod. 'Tell Hope we'll be back. If she asks where I'm gone, tell her I'm chasing up a lead about the two men in the photograph. I might have something.' Once he was sure that Ross acknowledged him, Macleod made his way out to the car park where Clarissa had pulled up at the entrance to the building, awaiting her boss.

The drive across town to a nursing home was completed with the snow falling down all around them. Macleod shivered inside the car and he looked at the thermostatic dial, noting that Clarissa had it just above the cold.

'Do you feel nothing?' he asked suddenly.

'What?'

'Do you feel nothing? Look at that temperature dial; it's bitter in here.'

'People say I have enough warmth in my life. Maybe I'm just too hot to handle, Seoras.'

Macleod shook his head. It had been different when he'd had Kirsten working on the team, a younger woman with probably too much respect for Macleod. However, he'd managed in one fell swoop to completely reverse the situation.

'Just be careful with this guy we're going to see. He's

awkward. He's probably not going to say much to me. Hopefully he will help.'

'You don't paint a great picture of him,' said Clarissa.

'There's not a great picture to paint, but he was a cop. He was an officer and as much as I didn't like his methods, he did at least go after the bad guys.'

'Was he dirty?' asked Clarissa.

'Oh, yes,' said Macleod. 'Very much so.'

They arrived at the nursing home on the far side of Inverness and crunched their way through the snow at the front door. They had to press a buzzer because the building was shut up. A member of staff in a green set of scrubs arrived and on production of their credentials, she let them into the home before letting them walk along a few corridors down to the room of the gentleman they'd asked for. On opening the door, Macleod saw a man lying on the bed with a mask attached to his face.

'He's on oxygen all the time at the moment. He's not got long to live, Inspector. Please don't upset him and generally just take it easy with him,' advised the staff member.

Macleod nodded and walked in, towards the bed. The man lying there reached up with a wrinkled hand and pulled the mask off his face. Macleod could see sunken eyes and grey hair that had almost disappeared but there was a grin that came across yellowing teeth.

'Macleod,' coughed the man. 'You bastard. You come to see me go down in the grave. I said it, didn't I?' The man coughed again. 'I said, Macleod, he'll put me six feet under.'

'I'm here, Angus, on business. I need your help.'

There was a splutter of coughs and intermixed laughs before the man started to reach over for a jug of water. Clarissa, seeing the man stretch and have difficulty in reaching, made her way over, poured a glass of water and then brought it up to the man's lips, helping him to drink it. Once he'd relaxed for a minute, the man looked back at Macleod.

'It's good to see you've got someone with a bit of manners. Urquhart, isn't it? You're the art filly.'

'I've dealt with them but I don't know you,' said Clarissa.

'Former Detective Inspector Angus Matheson, and while you don't remember me, I remember you. You were a lot younger then. You weren't exactly wild, but you were worth chasing.'

Clarissa looked over at Macleod. 'Is that all you guys do, detective inspectors? Just stare at us?'

For a moment Macleod looked affronted that Clarissa was even mentioning him in the same breath as this man. But then he ignored her and made his way over to Matheson. He plunked the photograph on the man's chest. Matheson reached over at his bedside, pressed a button and he was lifted up, the top end of the bed sliding into a position where Matheson was more upright.

'Get me my glasses, Macleod. Do something useful.'

With glasses in hand, Matheson stared and coughed at the photograph. 'Bloody hell,' he said. 'Seriously, what are you doing with these people?'

'I take it you know them, then,' said Macleod.

'You know one of them too. The guy on the right. He's to do with that TV station now. Making programmes or whatever. Back in the day he was handy with the drugs. He used to get me some stuff. It's bad for the nose, Clarissa. Bad for the—' The man coughed lately.

'It's just plain bad,' said Macleod. 'Enough with the reminiscing. Who's the other man?'

Matheson laughed and then coughed once more, having to turn around and grab a plastic cup to spit into. When he eventually found the voice to speak, he instead just laughed.

'Right in front of you, Macleod. You daft goat. You always were a right bollock, weren't you?'

'You can dispense with the insults,' said Macleod. 'I've got a killer on the loose.'

'Aye, you will have.' Matheson seemed to pull himself together somewhat. 'I hope it's not him. You see, Inspector Macleod, the man on the left's your current Superintendent.'

'No way,' said Clarissa, elated. 'Serious?'

'Aye. Back in those days he covered a lot up, but he used. Not just the drugs. He was right handy around a few women. You didn't get this photo off . . . no, not Janice. No way, not Janice. Is she still on the go? Oh, she was a woman. She was a woman and a half. Two right clowns of sons, like. Never knew who the dad was. My money was on Black.'

'My money's on him too,' said Macleod. 'What's the name of the other man, though?'

'John. John Douglas.'

Macleod nearly jumped. 'He's part of the TV crew. The producer,' said Macleod.

'Aye, he did well for himself once he cleaned his act up, though I'm not sure he did clean it up. I think he just went into personal use. That's what they call it, isn't it, when you're not dealing? It's just for recreation and personal use. Well, the personal use knocked the hell out of me,' and the man coughed deeply again. 'Now, go on, Macleod, you old bollock, you. Get your arse out of here unless you're here to watch me die. You'd love that, wouldn't you? Love that.'

'No,' said Macleod. 'I wouldn't.'

'Were you going to tell me then? Were you going to tell me about my maker? You're going to tell me about your precious religion.'

'I told you enough throughout your career,' said Macleod. 'It's your choice. Your choice.'

With that Macleod left the room and Clarissa was left standing. When she heard the man cough into a fit again and reach over for more water, she made her way to the cup and brought it to his lips. When she put the cup back down, the man grabbed her wrist.

'He's an old bollock,' the man said. 'God knows I hated him through the years, but you keep an eye on what he says, because he's usually bloody right.'

Chapter 22

On his return to the office, Macleod had gathered his team in, going over the evidence again, asking the question, 'Do we have enough to act on the Superintendent?' He made a request to the tech team on the basement level, asking who had accessed the various files over the last couple of months. It had come back showing the Superintendent's secretary's login.

Macleod wasn't convinced and sent Hope off to bring the woman into the station. For two hours, they quizzed her in his office until the woman eventually admitted that the Superintendent did in fact have her login. The trouble with everything was that it was circumstantial to a point. Macleod had lots of connections made but he couldn't prove any information had been handed over. As it came to the early hours of the morning, Macleod saw the dawn arrive and was still undecided about what to do.

'The way I see it, you've got to go for him,' said Clarissa. 'We need to put the brakes on him. Otherwise, he could just keep going, or worse still he could get to the end game, whatever that is.'

'The end game,' said Hope, 'surely has to be around Jeff

Danby. We still haven't found Owen.'

'No, we haven't,' said Macleod. 'I'm feeling there's going to be a play today as things are going to come to a head. The TV hasn't broadcast any more cases. There's no detail about specials coming up. There's just this march,' said Macleod. 'We should go and look for Karl Heinz again. I know he said he didn't want protection and he said he was going to hide out, but we should try and find him. Ross, Clarissa, can you get onto that?'

'What are you going to do, sir?' asked Ross.

'I'm going to confront our Superintendent. In fact, myself and Sergeant McGrath are going to arrest him. I think there's enough here. There's enough to hold him and keep him out of whatever mess is going on. That might be the more important point.'

His team dispersed and Macleod waited, looking out the window, his view of the car park now more important than ever. It was half past nine before he saw the superintendent arrive. Gordon Black stepped out of his Jaguar, walked a short distance over to the building and Macleod gave him two minutes to get to the top floor. Macleod had also advised the secretary not to come in today which meant the Detective Inspector was forced to knock on the door of the Superintendent's office.

'Come in.'

'I need to speak to you, Gordon.'

'About what, Macleod? Your people have been all over me. I had a word with your girl.'

Macleod had never heard Clarissa called a girl, and certainly not in that derogatory fashion. It was certainly a word he wouldn't use to her face.

'Oh, she's done a lot more digging, Gordon, a lot more digging. Do you recognise this photograph?' Macleod slapped the picture of the two men that Janice had given Hope on the desk.

'Where the hell did you get that? Just an old one from student days.'

'I've got a woman in Nairn tells me you plied her with drugs and used her, and I hear you're a father.'

Macleod saw the man's face retract quickly almost into panic before it became brazen again. 'Don't you spread these lies. You watch what you say, Macleod. You tread very carefully.'

'Is Jeff Danby your son?' asked Hope.

'He doesn't know,' said Macleod. 'Do you? You don't know because the two of you shared her. You shared Janice and maybe you shared her with others, I don't know. But there's two boys. Jeff's in prison. Was he too much like you?'

Gordon Black slammed his fist in the desk. 'You can take these damn lies out of here, Macleod. You can get out of this office. You start raking up this crap again and I'll break you. I am this force. I own the north up here. You understand that?'

'Is that because you own the media too? That's your friend there, isn't it? He's in the media and running a certain programme, isn't he? Producer for *Where Justice Fails*. Well, it's failed all right,' said Macleod. 'It's failed because it's let you loose to run the place.'

'What's your evidence, Macleod? What's your evidence?'

'Details of cases leaked across, details that were only in those files. It had to come from in here. It had to come from this station.'

'And have you found the leak? Did that little hound of yours find the leak?'

'Oh yes,' said Macleod, 'we found it. It's from that terminal out there.'

'Then you'd better arrest her. You better get hold of Deborah. Bring her in. You can throw her to the dogs for all I care.'

'We won't throw her anywhere,' said Hope. 'That's the tragedy of it; She protected your backside too. She was very confidential until pressed. You have her login, don't you?' said Macleod.

'No comment, Inspector,' said Black.

'What's going down today?' asked Macleod, beginning to pace the room. 'I want to know what's going to happen. Where's Owen?'

'Owen?'

'Yes, the other man that could be your son.' Hope glared indignantly at the man. He stared back at Hope.

'You don't have to go this way,' he said to her. 'Macleod's on his way out. Dinosaur. A fossil. He'll never make this stick. We'll kick him out of here. You can take over.' Black made his way round from behind the desk, came up close to Hope, putting an arm around her shoulder. 'I can make you something,' he said. 'Macleod's right. I've got the TV connections. You can be the person that cleans up Inverness. You could be the hero instead of hiding behind him again. You'd like that, wouldn't you?'

Hope lifted her arm and shoved Gordon Black's from her shoulder. 'Your shenanigans nearly cost me my man and I will follow that dinosaur over there a thousand miles further than I'd ever follow you.'

Macleod could see that Hope was straining, holding back.

'Your man,' said Black, 'probably doesn't know how to get hold of you. That's the thing these days, you don't know your place, do you? You don't know—'

'Sergeant McGrath,' said Macleod, 'place Gordon Black under arrest. Then cuff him, walk him down to the cells down below and tell the custody sergeant to hold him on my authority.'

'You've buried yourself this time, Macleod,' said Black, 'buried yourself. I have friends.'

'I have a killer,' said Macleod, now coming face to face with Black as Hope pulled the man's arms behind him, placing cuffs on them. 'If another one dies for you to cover your sorry arse, I will not rest until they put you away and then throw away the key. This place deserves better than scum like you.'

Macleod watched Hope take the man from the room and he noticed that she forced his arms up behind his back so that it hurt. He could hear her little apology every time she was, accidentally, too forceful.

'Hope, don't use the lift. Like I say, down the stairs, you can take him for a walk round some of the floors.'

Macleod was left alone in the office. He made his way over to the window, which unlike Macleod's, did not look down upon the car park. Instead, it looked over towards Raigmore Hospital. It made Macleod think about Hope's action within the hospital. Yes, John had been put at risk. Her man had been brave but also injured. Macleod needed to end this; he needed to find where it was going. For all his bravado, he was still struggling to bring it to a close.

Macleod made his way back down to his office where he switched on the TV and saw news reports of crowds gathering. It was only mid-morning, but he could see the tension on the streets. There were plenty of police officers around, but from where the camera crews were, it was difficult to tell how they were spread out.

Clarissa entered the office and give Macleod a smile.

'Oh, you've made some merry hell, haven't you?' she said. 'The station's all abuzz. Well, whoever's left in it. Most of the uniform are out on the street and I've heard there's plenty of crowds down.'

'How is it going out there?' asked Macleod.

'They're having difficulty. You've got the normal people out and about on their business and our people are trying to make sure they can go where they need to go, but down in the centre of the city, it's just bedlam. Protesters. They haven't formed an official march, so it's hard to police. There's been the odd scuffle already. The thing is, I heard that they're having trouble controlling the crowds.'

'Have they asked for any more support?'

'Oh, they've got support coming, Seoras. People across from Aberdeen, there's some heading on their way from Glasgow, but it's going to be a while before they're here. It seems that people are milling around the centre down towards the river. That seems to be the focus of everything. It's not like a normal protest.'

'What about the cameras?' asked Macleod. 'Do you know where they are?'

'Seems to be cameras everywhere. I've been watching the main news channels, and they're all coming up with their own news stories. But it's all just little highlights. There's no live footage, so to speak. Most of the normal channels are running their normal programmes. It's news source, but it's not big news. It's just big news for Inverness. Scottish bulletins are giving a bit more coverage, but that's it.'

'But there's a point to this. Jeff Danby is in prison; his

brother's missing. His brother, who Hope said was close to him—really close—couldn't handle it when Jeff went away. If Owen wants Jeff out, then he wants a groundswell of opinion to free him. He wants to put pressure on. That's what this is all about,' said Macleod suddenly. 'That's what it's all about, getting Jeff Danby out. All the other cases are irrelevant. They've all been picked to try and show injustice. Danby's case is secure, and that's the problem. They need this to be done on a groundswell of opinion, not about whether it's just or not, not about the evidence. Owen's created this, and where on earth is Owen?'

'You think Owen is behind the mask?' asked Clarissa. 'You reckon Owen's the Arbiter of Justice?'

'Don't use that word about him. More like arbitrary use of justice. Tell me more about what's going on down in the city.'

'I can't really say, Seoras. Like I say, the only one that's running completely live coverage is the *Where Justice Fails* programme. They've popped along for a special, but that was hardly surprising, was it? They've been driving most of this.'

'Let's get hold of the producer,' said Macleod. 'We've stayed away from them, but let's get hold of them.'

'To what end?' asked Clarissa. 'You said you were worried about giving them fuel. You were worried about engaging with them, but surely if we do this in the middle of this protest, that's all we'll do.'

'No,' said Macleod. 'Think about it. Think about the elements here. You've got a Superintendent that's reacted so late we haven't got enough people to man this protest. You've got someone who knows where to put all the cameras. If they're going to stage something, this is how you do it, and you've got Owen ready to take centre stage.'

'What are you thinking?' asked Clarissa. 'You don't reckon?'

'I do,' said Macleod. 'What's he done so far? He has filmed every killing. He has put every killing up on YouTube. What about doing it live with cameras there rolling? He's got the people to keep the police out. He's got a lack of police numbers due to Black downstairs. The stage is getting set. Have you had any luck finding Karl Heinz?'

Clarissa shook her head. 'Ross is still out with Nowak, but nothing. We tried to get uniform involved, but they're so busy.'

'Blast,' said Macleod. 'I never should have let him go on his own. The man was in trouble. The man—'

'You think?'

'If we don't find out why this is happening, Karl Heinz's time on this earth will be very short.'

Chapter 23

Macleod sat in the car with Hope beside him, her phone up on the dashboard, showing images from the *Where Justice Fails* live programme. Macleod had sent the rest of the team out to try and establish where the other TV cameras were because at the moment, the only image the channel was showing was from a street corner with packed crowds.

'If he's going to make a demonstration of it, if he's going to publicly make a statement,' said Macleod, 'he's going to need to get into the middle of the mass.'

'The crowds at the moment are down in the centre. They're filling up all the shopping streets, up the hill, past the castle, down across the bridge. Some are even spreading back out towards Eden Park. What about Eden Park, Seoras?'

'No, too hard to get away from, too hard to escape. We've got cars and vans. We've got people on the street. It might be a mass out there of protesters but if he's going to do what I think he'll do, all of them will be quite shocked and run.'

'They're out protesting already,' said Hope; 'they know what he's done. They know he's murdered people.'

'It's very different watching somebody murder someone on

a screen and most of them won't even have watched it. They'll just know about it. To see somebody do it for real, it's not the same, Hope. You know that. You've seen enough people die with me. It affects you in a different way, sticks with you.' Macleod saw her sombre face and knew she understood.

Macleod's phone rang and he picked it up, 'Macleod here.'

'Seoras, Clarissa. I've been all round the north side of the river. There's a couple of cameras facing in towards the city centre, one down by the music shop, another one up towards the castle. You don't think he's going to make a thing of it at the castle?'

'Hard to get out from though,' said Macleod. 'How do you escape from there? Also, hard for everyone to see. It's hidden away behind the shops. There's no platform to get up onto.'

'True,' said Clarissa, 'I can't see anywhere for him here. Ross is on the south side. Has he phoned in with anything yet?'

'Nothing,' said Macleod, 'nothing yet.' Macleod put the phone back down. 'I don't like this, Hope. It's getting too long. The parade's in full swing, the protest is flourishing. Why isn't he here? He should be in the middle of this now. This is when it's going to happen.'

'Patience, Seoras; as you always tell me, don't get worked up.'

'Somebody's life is on the line, Hope. I always get worked up. I just don't show it when I'm in front of the others.'

The phone rang again. 'Macleod.'

'It's Ross, Inspector. I've toured round the south side, it's blooming hard work. Everywhere is just choked up but the cameras, they're down streets, they're showing the crowd. There's a guy walking about with a camera on his shoulder, but he's interviewing the crowd. I can't see anywhere here that you would have a platform to be seen. There's so many people. He's going to want the cameras focused on him surely.'

'Exactly, Ross. Keep looking. You see anything unusual, you tell me, okay?'

'Of course, sir,' and the phone went dead again.

'Where is he, Hope?' said Macleod. 'Where is he?' Macleod stepped out of the car. They were outside of the main protest because Macleod wanted to be able to drive wherever he needed to be. If he was inside the crowds, it could be hard to get on the move; Conversely, getting inside would be difficult, as well.

'I haven't seen any change in the TV angles, Seoras. Look at those people; there's people dancing and singing.'

'As long as they're dancing and singing, that's fine.'

'Well, there's more than that. There are several scuffles going out. A few of our people have been injured, some badly.'

'Let's hope it doesn't kick off. It's hard enough trying to run a murder investigation. I'm not here to sanitise the city.'

'I'm sure our colleagues in uniform will be delighted about that.' Macleod shot a glance over at her, but Hope ignored him and stared at her phone screen. The phone rang again, and he picked his mobile up seeing it was PC Nowak. 'Andrea, Macleod, what is it?'

'Ross said I was to phone you, sir, if I felt it was important.'

'Of course,' said Macleod hurriedly, 'what is it?'

'I'm down by the river. I'm just looking from the bridge. There's a camera looking up the street towards the castle on the north side, on the south side there's one looking back away from the river, another one further down the river is looking into the streets as well, a similar one on the north side. That's four cameras, sir.'

'Okay,' said Macleod, 'and?'

'Don't you see? If you spun those cameras around, all four would be on the river.'

'The river,' shouted Macleod out loud, 'of course, he's going to go for the river. If you're on a boat in the river, everyone can watch you, it's going to be hard for us to get to him; he can do what he wants.'

Hope switched on the engine, 'He's going to need a boat, sir; he's going to have to come up in a boat. Surely, he'll come up from the Moray Firth side. He's not going to be coming down past the park.'

'Down at the marina—he could come in at the marina. Plenty of boats there—wouldn't look amiss. Wouldn't even look strange cruising out; could turn around and come up the river. If he's got a fairly big boat, he could get a reasonable platform on it. Hope, head for the marina.'

Macleod nearly fell over as Hope swung the car around, but he hung on as she headed off into the Inverness traffic.

'Nowak, stay there. You tell me if those cameras change.' He closed down the call and sent a text out to Clarissa and Ross advising them to head for the river.

'Grab my phone,' said Hope, as it fell off the dash. Macleod picked it up and stared at the programme in front of him. 'Hope, it has changed, those cameras have turned. She was right.'

'Let's hope we're not too late, Seoras,' said Hope putting her foot down. The car raced along towards the marina across from Kessock at the entrance to the Moray Firth. As they pulled up in the car park, they both jumped out leaving the doors open, running towards the marina. As they got closer, they slowed down surveying the boats.

'There,' said Macleod, and he pointed to a vessel just starting to move away.

'I can only see one person on board,' said Hope. She was staring at the white wheelhouse structure. But Macleod could see that below deck, there were several cabins. On the rear of the vessel, was a flat area from where people would fish, with several lockers which may have contained some of the fishing gear.

'We need to get onto that boat,' said Macleod.

'Well, we'll not catch him coming off the pier,' said Hope, 'and are we sure it's him?'

'The cameras are turned,' said Macleod, 'we've got to take the risk, come on.'

Together they ran off onto the marina and watched as the boat went down one set of pontoons. The boat would have to turn and come up another set before heading out into the Moray Firth. Macleod and Hope crouched down low and sprinted down between the boats and the second set of pontoons. The boat went round the end of them, and the pair got down tight behind one of the larger yachts, keeping themselves out of view.

'We can't jump in too quick,' said Macleod, 'if we do, we won't know where Karl Heinz is. He'll probably be on this boat, but we can't be sure. They may bring him on another one.'

'Then let's just get on the back,' said Hope, and she watched as the boat began to pull past the ends of the pontoons. There was one man in the wheelhouse looking forward, and Hope made a sprint, jumping onto the boat quickly. She landed gracefully and turned round holding an arm out. Macleod wasn't waiting, and he followed her, making the short jump, landing on the side of the boat, being pulled by Hope. The boat dipped slightly and Hope pushed the two of them behind the large lockers.

Hope heard the door of the wheelhouse open as the boat slowed down slightly. The man must have been looking out the back to see if anything was amiss, but then she heard the door close again. Hope raised her red head up above the lockers ever so slightly, and saw the man at the wheelhouse.

'Well, have we got the right boat?' asked Macleod quietly.

'There's a flag here,' said Hope. 'It's got the Lady Justice emblem on it; he's going to raise a flag,' said Hope.

'And he's going to kill Karl Heinz beneath it, you wait and see,' said Macleod; 'this is his centrepiece.'

'Do we move?' said Hope.

'No,' said Macleod, 'not until we see Karl Heinz. He won't kill him until he brings him up into his stage. We move too early, and he might dispatch him before, then just parade the body. If he's intending to parade the body, he will have killed him already.'

Hope nodded and kept low as the pair of them watched the marina disappear behind them. The boat made its way past the industrial docks and eventually into the River Ness making its way up towards the city centre. Macleod could start to see the road on either side, and the boat came to a gentle halt. The pair of them kept low. As the crowds on the other side gathered, looking inward, the wheelhouse door opened and Macleod peered around the side of the lockers to see a man in a mask come out, the Lady Justice emblem on his face. Behind him with a black hood on was another man, his hands tied behind his back.

Hope leaned close to Macleod, 'What's he doing with him?'

'I don't know, but be ready to move.'

The man in the mask produced a megaphone and turned to the crowd. 'You see before you Karl Heinz, a man who put Jeff Danby in jail. We will take revenge again, but the real justice will be when Jeff Danby is released. This case must be looked at or many more of these will follow. Let Jeff Danby be the example that corrects the many wrongs.'

The man from the wheelhouse came out with another man and together they began to tie rocks to Danby's feet. The Arbiter of Justice told him to move him to the side of the boat where they sat him down.

'They're going to tip him in, Hope. They're going to tip him in, drown him.' Macleod did not want to move too early as they were perfectly secreted between the edge of the boat and the lockers.

'We're going to put Karl Heinz in a permanent jail in the same way that he's locked up Jeff Danby.' There was a huge cheer from the crowd and Macleod couldn't believe his ears at the madness that was being stoked up. From the noise, he could hear scuffles, sirens in the distance, but he watched the arbiter step over.

'Now, Hope, now,' shouted Macleod. The pair of them raced out from behind the lockers. The arbiter took one look and shoved Karl Heinz. The man, still covered by a hood, tipped backwards, but the rocks that were attached to his feet caused him to remain on board, although he balanced precariously off the edge of it.

Macleod stepped forward and was assaulted by the wheelhouse man. He threw a punch catching Macleod on his shoulder. As Macleod buckled down, he reached forward, grabbing the man's leg before driving his shoulder right into his waist. The other man went to come across, and Macleod kicked out, hitting him on the ankle. It didn't stop the other man, simply slowed him down but it gave Hope a chance to reach the arbiter. She grabbed him, tussling, her hand reaching up to the man's mask.

With Hope's height, she was able to put one arm around the man as she sought to free the mask. It came off suddenly, and a face Hope had seen in a photograph from his mother appeared before her, but Owen Danby caught her unawares with a sharp punch to the jaw. Hope reeled backwards, falling onto her bottom. Owen Danby reached round, picked up one of the rocks, and threw it off the boat. Everything except the leg of Karl Heinz went overboard. Danby reached down again throwing the second rock and Karl Heinz began his descent into the river.

Macleod took a kick to the stomach, but he rolled to one side of the boat as best he could. 'Hope, get after Heinz, get Heinz.'

Macleod knew how experienced a swimmer Hope was and she didn't hesitate, pulling her jacket off as she lay on the ground. Owen Danby came across to her, but she let out an almighty kick straight between his legs, causing him to buckle over. She shoved him to one side and threw herself off into the water.

Macleod caught the foot of the next man coming over to kick him and bit into his leg, causing the man to yell and fall to the ground. As he got up, the other man made a move, but Macleod ducked a punch and caught him with a quick one to the stomach before running into the wheelhouse. He closed the door behind him, flicking a switch to lock it.

He then began to steer the boat over towards one side of

the river. As he looked out from the wheelhouse, he could see Clarissa at the riverside. Macleod's control of the boat was weak and he heard the two men banging on the door behind him. They were, however, thrown to one side as the boat collided with the river edge. Macleod fell himself, smacking his head off the side.

As he put a hand up, he could see the blood. He spun around to look at the door and through the glass, he saw Clarissa jumping down onto the boat. One of the men went to stand up, but although she was an older woman, Clarissa was merciless. He received a kick to the face and the next man received a kick to the stomach. She bent down, putting a handcuff on one and then slipping the other cuff onto the other man. Macleod tried to shout a warning as he saw Owen Danby stand up, but Clarissa had already pulled out a nightstick and whacked the man severely in the shins. He reared and she followed it up with another couple of strikes. In the next instance, PC Nowak was on board assisting Clarissa, taking the men to the ground. Macleod swooned, aware that this injury to his head was more than he'd thought it was. There was a rap at the door.

'Open the bloody door, Seoras.' It was Clarissa and Macleod stumbled forward, pulling back the latch before falling to the ground.

'Andrea, get the inspector.' Macleod was aware of Clarissa stepping over him and then the boat was on the move. 'Where the hell's Hope?' said Clarissa, 'We've got to find Hope.'

* * *

Hope was searching the murky depths. She'd been under the water for over a minute and knew she would surface soon, but she couldn't find anyone. Her eyes were open, but she could see nothing. Her hand touched something, and she brought her other hand into contact with it. It felt like a rock, but there was some sort of rope around it or a chain. It was rope!

She followed her hand along and then found a leg. She could feel her breath running out, but this was her man, surely. She needed to undo his knots to get him moving again, but Hope realised her breath would go. Quickly, she kicked for the surface, and as she broke it she looked around for the boat, but it was at the edge of the river now.

There was no time to shout to them so she ducked back down, reaching the bottom, scrambling around again before quickly finding the rock. She pulled at the rope, but it wouldn't come away. She'd have to get them off or the man would not move. She struggled for another thirty seconds, pulling at this rope, this way and that, but there was nothing. She reached down for the man's shoes, pulling them off, one after another, then tried moving the rope down his trousers, but they were too tight. They must have cut off the circulation, particularly, to his feet.

Hope realised she'd have to surface again, so up she went, breaking the water to find a boat on the move.

'Hope,' shouted Ross, 'have you found him? Have you found him?'

'I need a knife,' Hope shouted, gasping for breath, 'a knife.' She saw Ross running around the deck of the boat before entering the wheelhouse. The boat came over closer, almost too much and Hope had to move slightly, lest the boat crack her in the head. Then Ross was reaching over with a knife.

She didn't hesitate but stuck it between her teeth and dived. As she sought for the rock again, Hope found it and cut through the rope, where it was attached to the rock, and felt around to grab the man's other leg before taking that bind away as well. With both rocks removed, Hope pushed the man upwards, driving him up until she felt the weight of him break the surface and coming back on her, the buoyancy gone from underneath.

And then his weight was gone. Someone must have grabbed him up and onto the boat. Hope broke the surface and saw Ross reaching down with a hand. She shook her head.

'No, take him. I'm fine. Take him.'

The boat tore away to the side, and Hope could see the lights of ambulances in the distance, coming across the bridge to turn down the street towards them. She tried to float on her back, sucking in as much air as she could. Once she was happy she was stable, she swam over to the side. Hands reached down and helped her up onto the roadside. When she saw the first ambulance whizzing away, a second ambulance arrived and she saw a man being lifted onto a stretcher. She stumbled over. A medic had a cloth to a man's head, and she recognised the figure.

'Seoras,' she shouted, 'Seoras!' Arms wrapped around Hope.

'They've got him,' said Clarissa. 'They've got him.'

Chapter 24

Hope lay in bed and felt the arm wrapped around her. The previous night, she had drank a copious amount of wine, and when she'd stumbled into the bed, she just wanted the day to be gone. She was physically exhausted, but she'd also spent many hours in the hospital. It should have been a happy day for John was being discharged. A deeper cut would would've been serious, but the doctors had said it was recovering well, and they'd simply kept John in for another day to make sure he'd be okay. When he'd slipped into bed with her, he could only manage one arm around her. She said to him, 'You don't have to take care of me.' His simple words were that she was in a far worse state than he was.

She'd spent the time at the hospital, worried about Macleod. They were keeping him in overnight because of the bang on the head which had opened a deep wound, deep enough that they'd rushed him into A&E. True to form, he had recovered somewhat, and she left Jane in the hospital that night looking after her man. As long as there were no complications, as long as the injury didn't come back on him that night, he should be all right.

Karl Hines was a different matter. The man had been under

the water for a long time, but as much as Hope had saved him, they were worried about brain damage. He'd gone without oxygen for too long. It would be at least forty-eight hours before they had a clear idea about whether the man would recover well or not.

Hope grabbed the arm that was lying limply across her and pulled it close. It had been a while since she needed to be held. In the early hours of the morning, she found herself reflecting on the case. Macleod had taken a battering, but that was par for the course. He was an officer like her and expected it. She'd taken a good thump to the chin, but she was far younger than Seoras, able to handle the physical stuff. Clarissa had been a God-send though, jumping on board that boat, sorting out the people there and along with Ross and Nowak, they had secured the scene.

The news that night was full of the heroics of Hope McGrath. Of course, Macleod got his mention as one of the most visible policemen in Inverness, even if he didn't wish it. There were pictures of Hope being pulled out of the water, her tall six-foot frame looking like something from an action movie. She hadn't felt glamorous and she hadn't felt particularly good. All she'd done was what Macleod had told her to do—rescue their victim. It was he who had dealt with the others.

'They said you can get back in after eight o'clock,' said John behind her. 'I'm happy to go there with you. It's up to you what you want to do.'

'The biggest part of me wants to go and see him. Make sure he is all right, John, but if I could stay here and do it, I would.'

'What exactly is your relationship with him?' asked John. 'Are you sweet on him?'

'What do you mean?' asked Hope. 'I'm lying here without

anything on, in bed with you. I thought it was pretty obvious, you are my man of choice.'

'I didn't mean it that way,' said John. 'I mean, the man's twenty years older than you at least. You can still be sweet on someone. You don't have to want to climb into bed with him.'

'Then, I guess you're right,' said Hope. 'I'm very fond of him. I never thought I would be fond of someone like him. Come on. We'd best get up. I'll help you shower.'

'That sounds good,' said John, and he received a tap on his backside from Hope's free arm.

'In by eight,' she said. 'In by eight.'

* * *

Hope made her way with John to Raigmore Hospital where they took a lift up to the fifth floor. As the doors opened, she saw Clarissa Urquhart, the woman's eyes tired and bleary.

'Have you been here all night?' asked Hope.

'Well, somebody had to keep the team going. His nibs there getting cracked on the head, you sent home after all your efforts. I'm next in charge and no, I haven't been here all night. Down at the station for half of it with Ross. Even Nowak stayed until about eight o'clock. Then we had to send her home to look after her kids. We've done some initial statements and that, but to be honest,' yawned Clarissa, 'I'm absolutely knackered. Do you want a coffee?' she said to Hope.

'I'll go get them,' said John. Clarissa looked at the man with his arm in a sling. 'Are you one of these circus entertainers?' she asked. 'Because it's going to be quite a tray of coffee you bring up.'

'I will get them,' said John. 'Fill her in on what's been

happening as she's desperate to know.'

Hope looked round at John, tried to indicate that he didn't have to, but the man wouldn't have it. As he disappeared off to the lift again, Clarissa put her hand on Hope's shoulder.

'If you ever get rid of him, you send him to me.'

'And what would the man have done to deserve that?' said Hope.

'Touché,' said Clarissa. 'You'll be wanting to see the boss then. He's in that room over there. Jane's in with him. He's already asked for briefings about what's going on, but he's not allowed out of that room for another day.'

'How have things been?' asked Hope. 'I kind of went away into the hospital and really didn't see much of everything.'

'No, but you weren't in a state to anyway. The news reported very favourably for us. They talked about you a lot, how you prevented another death, Macleod's team being on top. It all sounded very good. They also got images of our superintendent being taken away. So, it's not all good from a police front. We also arrested the producer of the *Where Justice Fails* TV company. Oh, and Danby, once he'd been caught, sung like anything. He talked about what he was doing for his brother. The man was obsessional, not quite with it, but said he'd made his point.

'He doesn't know which of the two men are his father, Black, or the TV producer. I don't think he cares. He basically blackmailed them into helping him with the tales of his mother.'

'Well, Black deserved it' said Hope. 'Have things calmed down in town?'

'A lot of people who were out in that protest, they still grumped a bit, but it seems like they weren't prepared to follow a guy who was murdering for his brother. There was a lot of doubt put on whether or not any of the convictions were actually false. Police have announced a review, so we will have months of going back and forward about that, but everything's calming down,' said Clarissa. 'Give it two weeks, people will wonder what all the fuss was about.'

'Except Karl Hines,' said Hope. 'Any news?'

'No. Still in a coma. They're hoping he'll come out of it, but they don't know. But that's not your fault. You did well,' said Clarissa. 'He wouldn't have had a chance without you.'

Hope made her way towards Macleod's room, knocked lightly on the door, and opened it see Jane inside holding Macleod's hand. She got up immediately, walked over and threw her arms around Hope, having to reach up to the six-foot woman. Hope leaned down and hugged Jane tight.

'God love you, girl. Are you okay? Seoras told me about what you did. You have to teach him to swim. He's too quick to throw you in the water.'

Hope smiled. 'Well, that's the thing about him, isn't it? Always gets everybody else doing the dirty work.' She looked over and grinned at Macleod, who was sitting up in bed, and smiled at her.

'Now, now,' said Jane, 'just because I'm here, you don't have to keep your distance. Give him a hug.'

Hope let go of Jane, made her way quickly to Macleod, and threw her arms around him. 'I saw you in the ambulance; you had me bloody worried.'

'Just a bang on the head,' said Macleod. 'Everybody's getting overexcited, especially that woman there.'

'He's a horrible patient,' said Jane, 'I'm going to head home soon, leave him be except the staff here wouldn't have it. Said they needed somebody to keep him off their back.'

Hope laughed, stood up and looked down at Macleod. 'We got him,' she said. 'We did get him.'

'We got lucky. Not lucky enough. We don't know about Karl Hines.'

'I heard,' said Hope, 'but this was in the dark. This was a vigilante, Seoras. We started with nothing. Danby was darn good. Very clever, Owen Danby.'

'If he had some sort of a start in life, some sort of a father, he might have made something of himself,' said Macleod grumpily, while turning away. 'Look where our great Superintendent got him. Typical.'

'That's enough shop talk,' said Jane. 'You did it; you won. You're on top. The big win is the city's calming down. It got very nasty there for a while. The number of your colleagues shipping in downstairs,' Jane said to Seoras, 'isn't increasing anymore because of what you did. Now, shut up and be happy.'

'Get me out of the damn gown. I feel like my bare backside's on the bed.'

'Just shut up and take your medicine,' said Jane. She walked over, jumping up on the bed beside him and put her arm around him. 'I do actually love this guy—you do realise that, don't you?' she said to Hope. 'You're not going to get him from me.'

Hope grinned. She did have a fondness for Macleod, but she was so happy to see him with a woman who could handle him. There was a bump at the door, and she saw John standing there. It dawned on her suddenly he had one hand and it would have coffee in it, so she opened the door and in he came.

'I hope you're doing better, Inspector. I brought you one. I'm not sure how you take it.'

'Thank you,' said Macleod. Car-Hire-Man, isn't it?'

Hope shot a look at Macleod, but John simply smiled. 'John. I hope you're feeling better.'

'Seoras, and I'm not doing too bad, thank you. Just promise me you'll take care of that woman.'

'Can everybody just give us a minute?' asked Hope. 'There's something I want to clear up with the inspector.'

Jane and John looked quickly at each other, and then they took their coffee and stepped aside.

'What's the matter?' asked Macleod. 'It can't be much more about the case you want to know. Besides, Clarissa will cover all that for you.'

'Is it worth it?' said Hope.

'Is what worth it?' asked Macleod.

'This job. You've nearly lost Jane before. I nearly lost John.'

'He chose you. This is what you are. If you stopped being a detective and went to be with him like that, you'd be half the woman you are to him. Now, shut up and get on with it.'

Hope stared at him. 'Do you know something I realised today, Seoras? I'm quite fond of you in a strange way, but you really can put people off you sometimes.'

Macleod laughed. 'Open that door and let them in.'

Hope made her way back to the door, opened it and found Clarissa walking through with Ross and Nowak as well.

'Ah, the cavalry's here,' said Macleod. 'While everyone is here, can I say something?'

'Oh heck, he's going to make a speech,' said Clarissa.

'Now, now,' said Macleod, 'I just want to say, we wouldn't have got anywhere with this except for that woman there. Clarissa, you did well. You stuck to your guns in front of Black.'

For a moment, Clarissa looked like she didn't know what to say and she just smiled. 'Thank you, Inspector. Thank you very much.'

Hope watched the two of them exchange a grin and then Ross burst forward. 'I know this is a very tender moment,' he said, 'and it's great to see but can I just show everybody something?'

The group turned and stared at him. From behind his back, he produced a T-shirt, and held it up. Macleod stared at it. It was white and there was a picture of Lady Justice on it. There was no red forbidden sign around her but instead, where Lady Justice's face would've been, superposed was an image of Macleod.

'I thought I could get one for all of the team,' said Ross laughing. 'You finally hit the big time, sir. You're a hero. Macleod brought safety back to Inverness.'

Macleod could tell the edge in Ross's voice. He wasn't sure if he'd gone too far, but Macleod called him over.

'Let me see that properly.' Macleod held the T-shirt in front of him and Hope made her way over, putting her arm on his shoulder. 'See, Seoras, you've hit the big time.'

'I look at this, Hope, and there's only one time I think about; Time to flipping retire.'

Read on to discover the Patrick Smythe series!

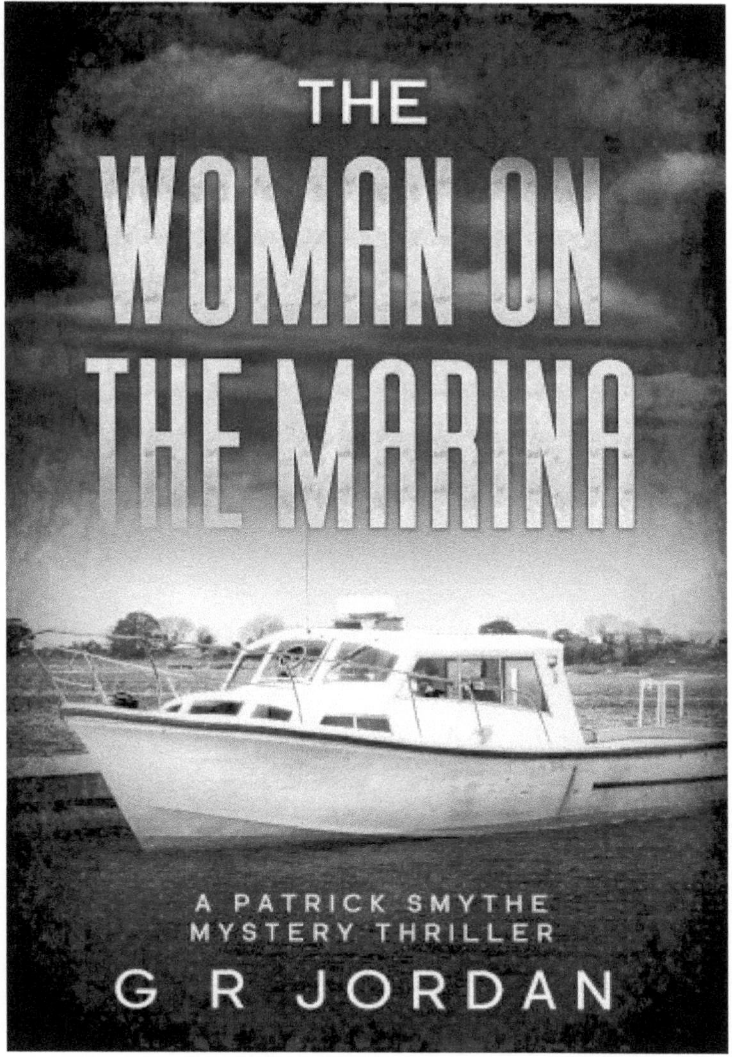

Start your Patrick Smythe journey here!

Patrick Smythe is a former Northern Irish policeman who

after suffering an amputation after a bomb blast, takes to the sea between the west coast of Scotland and his homeland to ply his trade as a private investigator. Join Paddy as he tries to work to his own ethics while knowing how to bend the rules he once enforced. Working from his beloved motorboat 'Craigantlet', Paddy decides to rescue a drug mule in this short story from the pen of G R Jordan.

Join G R Jordan's monthly newsletter about forthcoming releases and special writings for his tribe of avid readers and then receive your free Patrick Smythe short story.

Go to https://bit.ly/PatrickSmythe for your Patrick Smythe journey to start!

About the Author

GR Jordan is a self-published author who finally decided at forty that in order to have an enjoyable lifestyle, his creative beast within would have to be unleashed. His books mirror that conflict in life where acts of decency contend with self-promotion, goodness stares in horror at evil, and kindness blindsides us when we at our worst. Corrupting our world with his parade of wondrous and horrific characters, he highlights everyday tensions with fresh eyes whilst taking his methodical, intelligent mainstays on a roller-coaster ride of dilemmas, all the while suffering the banter of their provocative sidekicks.

A graduate of Loughborough University where he masqueraded as a chemical engineer but ultimately played American football, Gary had worked at changing the shape of cereal flakes and pulled a pallet truck for a living. Watching vegetables freeze at -40'C was another career highlight and he was also one of the Scottish Highlands "blind" air traffic controllers.

These days he has graduated to answering a telephone to people in trouble before telephoning other people to sort it out.

Having flirted with most places in the UK, he is now based in the Isle of Lewis in Scotland where his free time is spent between raising a young family with his wife, writing, figuring out how to work a loom and caring for a small flock of chickens. Luckily, his writing is influenced by his varied work and life experience as the chickens have not been the poetical inspiration he had hoped for!

You can connect with me on:

https://grjordan.com

https://facebook.com/carpetlessleprechaun

Subscribe to my newsletter:

https://bit.ly/PatrickSmythe

Also by G R Jordan

G R Jordan writes across multiple genres including crime, dark and action adventure fantasy, feel good fantasy, mystery thriller and horror fantasy. Below is a selection of his work. Whilst all books are available across online stores, signed copies are available at his personal shop.

The Cortado Club (Highlands & Islands Detective Book 17)
https://grjordan.com/product/the-cortado-club
An established coffee house with a reputation for excellence. A rapid surge in customers dying with froth on their lips. Can Macleod and McGrath discover the link between the clientele before the last cup is drunk?

When Macleod is called back to his Isle of Lewis roots, he finds the most sedate murders he has ever known. But for all the quietness and beauty in the method of dispatch, an evil seeks to destroy the community. With a subtlety Macleod finds hard to expose, the killer follows their path of perfect destruction. Can the Inspector discover his most taxing nemesis yet?

Why take two shots when one will do?

The Nationalist Express (Kirsten Stewart Thrillers #4)
https://grjordan.com/product/the-nationalist-express
A country divided by a historic vote. The whisper of a bombing amongst the loyal few. Can Kirsten infiltrate an extreme nationalist agenda and prevent a disaster south of the border?

Scotland is once again in political turmoil as it returns to the debate of whether to remain part of the United Kingdom. Under all the paraphernalia of various vying parties, Kirsten and her team discover a scheme to promote the separation from the Union with a series of terrorist plots. And when London becomes the target, the stakes are raised significantly. Can the recently formed team remain impartial while bringing the nefarious scheme to light?

What does history matter when you can fix the future?

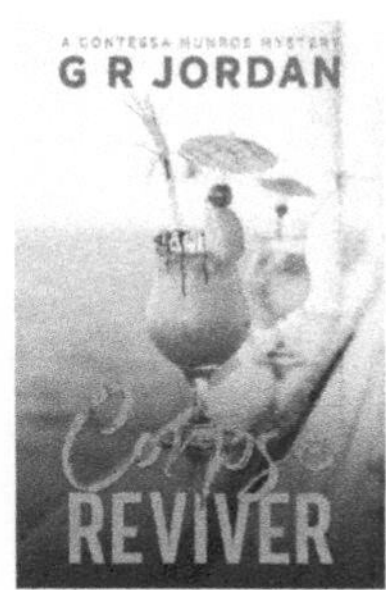

Corpse Reviver (A Contessa Munroe Mystery #1)

https://grjordan.com/product/corspe-reviver

A widowed Contessa flees to the northern waters in search of adventure. An entrepreneur dies on an ice pack excursion. But when the victim starts moonlighting from his locked cabin, can the Contessa uncover the true mystery of his death?

Catriona Cullodena Munroe, widow of the late Count de Los Palermo, has fled the family home, avoiding the scramble for title and land. As she searches for the life she always wanted, the Contessa, in the company of the autistic and rejected Tiff, must solve the mystery of a man who just won't let his business go.

Corpse Reviver is the first murder mystery involving the formidable and sometimes downright rude lady of leisure and her straight talking niece. Bonded by blood, and thrown together by fate, join this pair of thrill seekers as they realise that flirting with danger brings a price to pay.

Highlands and Islands Detective Thriller Series
https://grjordan.com/product/waters-edge

Join stalwart DI Macleod and his burgeoning new DC McGrath as they look into the darker side of the stunningly scenic and wilder parts of the north of Scotland. From the Black Isle to Lewis, from Mull to Harris and across to the small Isles, the Uists and Barra, this mismatched pairing follow murders, thieves and vengeful victims in an effort to restore tranquillity to the remoter parts of the land.

Be part of this tale of a surprise partnership amidst the foulest deeds and darkest souls who stalk this peaceful and most beautiful of lands, and you'll never see the Highlands the same way again

The Disappearance of Russell Hadleigh (Patrick Smythe Book 1)
https://grjordan.com/product/the-disappearance-of-russell-hadleigh

A retired judge fails to meet his golf partner. His wife calls for help while running a fantasy play ring. When Russians start co-opting into a fairly-traded clothing brand, can Paddy untangle the strands before the bodies start littering the golf course?

In his first full novel, Patrick Smythe, the single-armed former policeman, must infiltrate the golfing social scene to discover the fate of his client's husband. Assisted by a young starlet of the greens, Paddy tries to understand just who bears a grudge and who likes to play in the rough, culminating in a high stakes showdown where lives are hanging by the reaction of a moment. If you love pacey action, suspicious motives and devious characters, then Paddy Smythe operates amongst your kind of people.

Love is a matter of taste but money always demands more of its suitor.

Surface Tensions (Island Adventures Book 1)

https://grjordan.com/product/surface-tensions

Mermaids sighted near a Scottish island. A town exploding in anger and distrust. And Donald's got to get the sexiest fish in town, back in the water.

"Surface Tensions" is the first story in a series of Island adventures from the pen of G R Jordan. If you love comic moments, cosy adventures and light fantasy action, then you'll love these tales with a twist. Get the book that amazon readers said, "perfectly captures life in the Scottish Hebrides" and that explores "human nature at its best and worst".

Something's stirring the water!

Lightning Source UK Ltd.
Milton Keynes UK
UKHW011226290722
406567UK00001B/388